Selected

CHARLES DICKENS

RUPA

Published by
Rupa Publications India Pvt. Ltd 2014
7/16, Ansari Road, Daryaganj
New Delhi 110002

Sales Centres:
Allahabad Bengaluru Chennai
Hyderabad Jaipur Kathmandu
Kolkata Mumbai

ISBN: 978-81-291-3147-8

First impression 2014

10 9 8 7 6 5 4 3 2 1

Printed at Shree Maitrey Printech Pvt. Ltd., Noida

Selected Stories by
CHARLES DICKENS

Books in this Series:

Selected Stories by O. Henry

Selected Stories by Anton Chekhov

Selected Stories by Guy de Maupassant

Selected Stories by Mark Twain

Selected Stories by Edgar Allan Poe

Selected Stories by Rudyard Kipling

Selected Stories by Saki

Selected Stories by Oscar Wilde

Selected Stories by Honoré de Balzac

Selected Stories by Charles Dickens

Selected Stories by D.H. Lawrence

Selected Stories by H.G. Wells

Selected Stories by Jack London

Selected Stories by Joseph Conrad

Selected Stories by Leo Tolstoy

Selected Stories by Sir Arthur Conan Doyle

CONTENTS

INTRODUCTION

Charles John Huffam Dickens (7 February 1812–9 June 1870) was an English writer and social critic. He created some of the world's most memorable fictional characters. During his life, his works enjoyed unprecedented fame, and by the twentieth century his literary genius was broadly acknowledged by critics and scholars. His novels and short stories continue to be widely popular.

Over a period of twenty years Dickens wrote fifteen novels, five novellas and hundreds of short stories. He campaigned vigorously for children's rights, education and other social reforms.

Dickens is relevant even today. The human story has hardly changed. We may have tablets and smartphones now but people are still working on miserable wages as they manufacture goods. Exploitation of child labourers is still a reality in some countries. The bleak times represented in his works are just as relevant in today's world. We still live in Dickensian times.

- 'A Child's Dream of a Star' is a touching story of a brother and sister who wait every night for the stars to come out. But after a series of events, the child loses his family, including his sister.
- 'The Signal-Man' tells the narrator of a ghost that has been haunting him. Each spectral appearance precedes a tragic event on the railway on which the signalman works.
- In 'The Trial for Murder', a victim's ghost takes a seat in the jury at the trial of his killer.

at the trial of his killer.

- In 'Hunted Down', the astute Sampson suspects that a certain Mr Julius Slinkton, who turns up in his office one morning, is not all that he seems. As Slinkton crops up more and more frequently in Sampson's life, he realizes that a monstrous crime is about to be committed.
- 'Doctor Marigold', named for the man who delivered him, is a 'cheap-jack' who hawks sundries from a travelling cart. He inhabits with his wife and his daughter, Sophy. The mother beats Sophy, but Marigold, feeling powerless, does nothing to stop her. When the child dies of a fever, her guilt-wracked mother commits suicide.
- 'George Silverman's Explanation' is about Silverman, who is born in a Preston cellar, and spends his early years locked in there, often left alone while his parents go out to seek work, or to somehow scrape money together.
- 'The Baron of Grogswig' lived in an old castle in Germany. Strange sounds and light effects within the castle were blamed on the ghost of a traveller who had been murdered by one of the baron's ancestors. He decided to marry a fellow Baron's daughter. What happens next?

1

A CHILD'S DREAM OF A STAR

There was once a child, and he strolled about a good deal, and thought of a number of things. He had a sister, who was a child, too, and his constant companion. These two used to wonder all day long. They wondered at the beauty of the flowers; they wondered at the height and blueness of the sky; they wondered at the depth of the bright water; they wondered at the goodness and the power of God who made the lovely world.

They used to say to one another sometimes, supposing all the children upon earth were to die, would the flowers, and the water, and the sky be sorry? They believed they would be sorry. For, said they, the buds are the children of the flowers, and the little playful streams that gambol down the hillsides are the children of the water; and the smallest bright specks playing at hide-and-seek in the sky all night, must surely be the children of the stars; and they would all be grieved to see their playmates, the children of men, no more.

There was one clear shining star that used to come out in the sky before the rest, near the church spire, above the graves. It was larger and more beautiful, they thought, than all others, and every night they watched for it, standing hand in hand at the window. Whoever saw it first, cried out, 'I see the star!' And often they cried out both together, knowing so well when it would rise, and where.

So they grew to be such friends with it, that before lying down in their beds, they always looked out once again, to bid it good night; and when they were turning around to sleep, they used to say, 'God bless the star!'

But while she was very young, oh, very, very young, the sister drooped, and came to be so weak that she could no longer stand in the window at night; and then the child looked sadly out by himself, and when he saw the star, turned round and said to the patient, pale face on the bed, 'I see the star!' and then a smile would come upon the face, and a little weak voice used to say, 'God bless my brother and the star!'

And so the time came, all too soon! When the child looked out alone, and when there was no face on the bed; and when there was a little grave among the graves, not there before; and when the star made long rays down toward him, as he saw it through his tears.

Now, these rays were so bright, and they seemed to make such a shining way from earth to heaven, that when the child went to his solitary bed, he dreamed about the star; and dreamed that, lying where he was, he saw a train of people taken up that sparkling road by angels. And the star, opening, showed him a great world of light, where many more such angels waited to receive them.

All these angels who were waiting turned their beaming eyes upon the people who were carried up into the star; and some came out from the long rows in which they stood, and fell upon the people's necks, and kissed them tenderly, and went away with them down avenues of light, and were so happy in their company, that lying in his bed he wept for joy.

But there were many angels who did not go with them, and among them one he knew. The patient face that once had lain upon the bed was glorified and radiant, but his heart found out his sister among all the host.

His sister's angel lingered near the entrance of the star, and said to the leader among those who had brought the people thither—

'Is my brother come?'

And he said, 'No.'

She was turning hopefully away, when the child stretched out his arms, and cried, 'O sister, I am here! Take me!' And then she turned her beaming eyes upon him and it was night; and the star was shining into the room, making long rays down toward him as he saw it through his tears.

From that hour forth the child looked out upon the star as on the home he was to go to, when his time should come; and he thought that he did not belong to the earth alone, but to the star too, because of his sister's angel gone before.

There was a baby born to be a brother to the child; and while he was so little that he never yet had spoken word, he stretched his tiny form out on his bed and died.

Again the child dreamed of the opened star, and of the company of angels, and the train of people, and the rows of angels with their beaming eyes all turned upon those people's faces.

Said his sister's angel to the leader: 'Is my brother come?'

And he said, 'Not that one, but another.'

As the child beheld his brother's angel in her arms, he cried: 'O sister, I am here! Take me!' And she turned and smiled upon him, and the star was shining.

He grew to be a young man, and was busy at his books, when an old servant came to him and said:—

'Thy mother is no more. I bring her blessing on her darling son!'

Again at night he saw the star, and all that former company. Said his sister's angel to the leader:—

'Is my brother come?'

And he said, 'Thy mother!'

A mighty cry of joy went forth through all the star, because the mother was reunited to her two children. And he stretched out his arms and cried: 'O mother, sister, and brother, I am here! Take me!' And they answered him, 'Not yet.' And the star was shining.

He grew to be a man whose hair was turning gray, and he was sitting in his chair by the fireside, heavy with grief, and with his face bedewed with tears, when the star opened once again.

Said his sister's angel to the leader, 'Is my brother come?'

And he said, 'Nay, but his maiden daughter.'

And the man who had been the child saw his daughter, newly lost to him, a celestial creature among those three, and he said, 'My daughter's head is on my sister's bosom, and her arm is round my mother's neck, and at her feet there is the baby of old time, and I can bear the parting from her, God be praised!'

And the star was shining.

Thus the child came to be an old man, and his once smooth face was wrinkled, and his steps were slow and feeble, and his back was bent. And one night as he lay upon his bed, his children standing round, he cried, as he had cried so long ago: 'I see the star!'

They whispered to one another, 'He is dying.'

And he said: 'I am. My age is falling from me like a garment, and I move toward the star as a child. And, O my Father, now I thank thee that it has so often opened to receive those dear ones who await me!'

And the star was shining; and it shines upon his grave.

2

THE SIGNAL-MAN

'Halloa! Below there!'

When he heard a voice thus calling to him, he was standing at the door of his box, with a flag in his hand, furled round its short pole. One would have thought, considering the nature of the ground, that he could not have doubted from what quarter the voice came; but, instead of looking up to where I stood on the top of the steep cutting nearly over his head, he turned himself about and looked down the Line. There was something remarkable in his manner of doing so, though I could not have said, for my life, what. But, I know it was remarkable enough to attract my notice, even though his figure was foreshortened and shadowed, down in the deep trench, and mine was high above him, so steeped in the glow of an angry sunset that I had shaded my eyes with my hand before I saw him at all.

'Halloa! Below!'

From looking down the Line, he turned himself about again, and, raising his eyes, saw my figure high above him.

'Is there any path by which I can come down and speak to you?'

He looked up at me without replying, and I looked down at him without pressing him too soon with a repetition of my idle question. Just then, there came a vague vibration in the earth and air, quickly changing into a violent pulsation, and an oncoming rush that caused me to start back, as though it had force to draw me down. When such vapour as rose to my height from this rapid train, had passed me and was skimming away over the landscape, I looked down again, and saw him refurling the flag he had shown while the train went by.

I repeated my inquiry. After a pause, during which he seemed to regard me with fixed attention, he motioned with his rolled-up flag towards a point on my level, some two or three hundred yards distant. I called down to him, 'All right!' and made for that point. There, by dint of looking closely about me, I found a rough zig-zag descending path notched out which I followed.

The cutting was extremely deep, and unusually precipitate. It was made through a clammy stone that became oozier and wetter as I went down. For these reasons, I found the way long enough to give me time to recall a singular air of reluctance or compulsion with which he had pointed out the path.

When I came down low enough upon the zig-zag descent, to see him again, I saw that he was standing between the rails on the way by which the train had lately passed, in an attitude as if he were waiting for me to appear. He had his left hand at his chin, and that left elbow rested on his right hand crossed over his breast. His attitude was one of such expectation and watchfulness that I stopped a moment, wondering at it.

I resumed my downward way, and, stepping out upon the level of the railroad and drawing nearer to him, saw that he was a dark sallow man, with a dark beard and rather heavy eyebrows. His post was in as solitary and dismal a place as ever I saw. On either side, a dripping-wet wall of jagged stone, excluding all view but a strip of sky; the perspective one way, only a crooked prolongation of this great dungeon; the shorter perspective in the other direction, terminating in a gloomy red light, and the gloomier entrance to a black tunnel, in whose massive architecture there was a barbarous, depressing, and forbidding air. So little sunlight ever found its way to this spot, that it had an earthy deadly smell; and so much cold wind rushed through it, that it struck chill to me, as if I had left the natural world.

Before he stirred, I was near enough to him to have touched him. Not even then removing his eyes from mine, he stepped back one step, and lifted his hand.

This was a lonesome post to occupy (I said), and it had riveted my attention when I looked down from up yonder. A visitor was a rarity, I should suppose; not an unwelcome rarity, I hoped? In me, he merely saw a man who had been shut up within narrow limits all his life, and who, being at last set free, had a newly awakened interest in these great works. To such purpose I spoke to him; but I am far from sure of the terms I used, for, besides that I am not happy in opening any conversation, there was something in the man that daunted me.

He directed a most curious look towards the red light near the tunnel's mouth, and looked all about it, as if something were missing from it, and then looked at me.

That light was part of his charge? Was it not?

He answered in a low voice: 'Don't you know it is?'

The monstrous thought came into my mind as I perused the fixed eyes and the saturnine face, that this was a spirit, not a man. I have speculated since, whether there may have been infection in his mind.

In my turn, I stepped back. But in making the action, I detected in his eyes some latent fear of me. This put the monstrous thought to flight.

'You look at me,' I said, forcing a smile, 'as if you had a dread of me.'

'I was doubtful,' he returned, 'whether I had seen you before.'

'Where?'

He pointed to the red light he had looked at.

'There?' I said.

Intently watchful of me, he replied (but without sound), Yes.

'My good fellow, what should I do there? However, be that as it may, I never was there, you may swear.'

'I think I may.' he rejoined. 'Yes. I am sure I may.'

His manner cleared, like my own. He replied to my remarks with readiness, and in well-chosen words. Had he much to do there? Yes; that was to say, he had enough responsibility to bear; but exactness and watchfulness were what was required of him, and of actual work—manual labour he had next to none. To change that signal, to trim those lights, and to turn this iron handle now and then, was all he had to do under that head. Regarding those many long and lonely hours of which I seemed to make so much, he could only say that the routine of his life had shaped itself into that form, and he had grown used to it. He had taught himself a language down here—if only to know it by sight, and to have formed his own crude ideas of its pronunciation, could be called learning it. He had also worked at fractions and decimals, and tried a little algebra; but he was, and had been as a boy, a poor hand at figures. Was it necessary for him when on duty, always to remain in that channel of damp air, and could he never rise into the sunshine from between those high stone walls? Why, that depended upon times and circumstances. Under some conditions there would be less upon the Line than under others, and the same held good as to certain hours of the day and night. In bright weather, he did choose occasions for getting a little above these lower shadows; but, being at all times liable to be called by his electric bell, and at such times listening for it with redoubled anxiety, the relief was less than I would suppose.

He took me into his box, where there was a fire, a desk for an official book in which he had to make certain entries, a telegraphic instrument with its dial face and needles, and the little bell of which he had spoken. On my trusting that he would excuse the remark that he had been well-educated, and (I hoped I might say without offence), perhaps educated above that station, he observed that instances of slight incongruity in such-wise would rarely be found wanting among large bodies of men; that he had heard it was so in workhouses, in the police force, even in that last desperate resource, the army; and that he knew it was so, more or less, in any great railway staff. He had been, when young (if I could believe it, sitting in that, hut; he scarcely could), a student of natural philosophy, and had attended lectures; but he had run wild, misused his opportunities, gone down, and never risen again. He had no complaint to offer about that. He had made his bed and he lay upon it. It was far too late to make another.

All that I have here condensed, he said in a quiet manner, with his grave dark regards divided between me and the fire. He threw in the word 'Sir' from time to time, and especially when he referred to his youth; as though to request me to understand that he claimed to be nothing but what I found him. He was several times interrupted by the little bell, and had to read off messages, and send replies. Once, he had to stand without the door, and display a flag as a train passed, and make some verbal communication to the driver. In the discharge of his duties I observed him to be remarkably exact and vigilant, breaking off his discourse at a syllable, and remaining silent until what he had to do was done.

In a word, I should have set this man down as one of the safest of men to be employed in that capacity, but for the circumstance that while he was speaking to me he twice broke off with a fallen colour, turned his face towards the little bell when it did NOT ring, opened the door of the hut (which was kept shut to exclude the unhealthy damp), and looked out towards the red light near the mouth of the tunnel. On both of those occasions, he came back to the fire with the inexplicable air upon him which I had remarked, without being able to define, when we were so far as under.

Said I when I rose to leave him: 'You almost make me think

that I have met with a contented man.'

(I am afraid I must acknowledge that I said it to lead him on.)

'I believe I used to be so,' he rejoined, in the low voice in which he had first spoken; 'but I am troubled, sir, I am troubled.'

He would have recalled the words, if he could. He had said them, however, and I took them up quickly.

'With what? What is your trouble?'

'It is very difficult to impart, sir. It is very, very difficult to speak of. If ever you make me another visit, I will try to tell you.'

'But I expressly intend to make you another visit. Say, when shall it be?'

'I go off early in the morning, and I shall be on again at ten tomorrow night, sir.'

'I will come at eleven.'

He thanked me, and went out at the door with me. 'I'll show my white light, sir,' he said, in his peculiar low voice, 'till you have found the way up. When you have found it, don't call out! And when you are at the top, don't call out!'

His manner seemed to make the place strike colder to me, but I said no more than 'Very well.'

'And when you come down tomorrow night, don't call out! Let me ask you a parting question. What made you cry 'Halloa! Below there!' tonight?'

'Heaven knows,' said I. 'I cried something to that effect——'

'Not to that effect, sir. Those were the very words. I know them well.'

'Admit those were the very words. I said them, no doubt, because I saw you below.'

'For no other reason?'

'What other reason could I possibly have!'

'You had no feeling that they were conveyed to you in any supernatural way?'

'No.'

He wished me good night, and held up his light. I walked by the side of the down line of rails (with a very disagreeable sensation of a train coming behind me), until I found the path. It was easier to mount than to descend, and I got back to my inn without any adventure.

Punctual to my appointment, I placed my foot on the first notch of the zig-zag next night, as the distant clocks were striking eleven. He was waiting for me at the bottom, with his white light on. 'I have not called out,' I said, when we came close together; 'May I speak now?' 'By all means, sir.' 'Good night then, and here's my hand.' 'Good night, sir, and here's mine.' With that, we walked side by side to his box, entered it, closed the door, and sat down by the fire.

'I have made up my mind, sir,' he began, bending forward as soon as we were seated, and speaking in a tone but a little above a whisper, 'that you shall not have to ask me twice what troubles me. I took you for someone else yesterday evening. That troubles me.'

'That mistake?'

'No. That someone else.'

'Who is it?'

'I don't know.'

'Like me?'

'I don't know. I never saw the face. The left arm is across the face, and the right arm is waved. Violently waved. This way.'

I followed his action with my eyes, and it was the action of an arm gesticulating with the utmost passion and vehemence: 'For God's sake clear the way!'

'One moonlight night,' said the man, 'I was sitting here, when I heard a voice cry 'Halloa! Below there!' I started up, looked from that door, and saw this someone else standing by the red light near the tunnel, waving as I just now showed you. The voice seemed hoarse with shouting, and it cried, 'Look out! Look out!' And then again 'Halloa! Below there! Look out!' I caught up my lamp, turned it on red, and ran towards the figure, calling, 'What's wrong? What has happened? Where?' It stood just outside the blackness of the tunnel. I advanced so close upon it that I wondered at its keeping the sleeve across its eyes. I ran right up at it, and had my hand stretched out to pull the sleeve away, when it was gone.'

'Into the tunnel.' said I.

'No. I ran into the tunnel, five hundred yards. I stopped and held my lamp above my head, and saw the figures of the measured distance, and saw the wet stains stealing down the walls and trickling through the arch. I ran out again, faster than I had run in (for I had a mortal abhorrence of the place upon me), and I looked all round the red light with my own red light, and I went up the iron ladder to the gallery atop of it, and I came down again, and ran back here. I telegraphed both ways, 'An alarm has been given. Is anything wrong?' The answer came back, both ways: 'All well.''

Resisting the slow touch of a frozen finger tracing out my spine, I showed him how that this figure must be a deception of his sense of sight, and how that figures, originating in disease of the delicate nerves that minister to the functions of the eye, were known to have often troubled patients, some of whom had become conscious of the nature of their affliction, and had even proved it by experiments upon themselves. 'As to an imaginary cry,' said I, 'do but listen for a moment to the wind in this unnatural valley while we speak so low, and to the wild harp it makes of the telegraph wires!'

That was all very well, he returned, after we had sat listening for a while, and he ought to know something of the wind and the wires, he who so often passed long winter nights there, alone and watching. But he would beg to remark that he had not finished.

I asked his pardon, and he slowly added these words, touching my arm:

'Within six hours after the Appearance, the memorable accident on this line happened, and within ten hours the dead and wounded were brought along through the tunnel over the spot where the figure had stood.'

A disagreeable shudder crept over me, but I did my best against it. It was not to be denied, I rejoined, that this was a remarkable coincidence, calculated deeply to impress his mind. But it was unquestionable that remarkable coincidences did continually occur, and they must be taken into account in dealing with such a subject. Though to be sure I must admit, I added (for I thought I saw that he was going to bring the objection to bear upon me), men of common sense did not allow much for coincidences in making the ordinary calculations of life.

He again begged to remark that he had not finished.

I again begged his pardon for being betrayed into interruptions.

'This,' he said, again laying his hand upon my arm, and glancing over his shoulder with hollow eyes, 'was just a year ago. Six or seven months passed, and I had recovered from the surprise and shock, when one morning, as the day was breaking, I, standing at that door, looked towards the red light, and saw the spectre again.' He stopped, with a fixed look at me.

'Did it cry out?'

'No. It was silent.'

'Did it wave its arm?'

'No. It leaned against the shaft of the light, with both hands before the face. Like this.'

Once more, I followed his action with my eyes. It was an action of mourning. I have seen such an attitude in stone figures on tombs.

'Did you go up to it?'

'I came in and sat down, partly to collect my thoughts, partly because it had turned me faint. When I went to the door again, daylight was above me, and the ghost was gone.'

'But nothing followed? Nothing came of this?'

He touched me on the arm with his forefinger twice or thrice, giving a ghastly nod each time:

'That very day, as a train came out of the tunnel, I noticed, at a carriage window on my side, what looked like a confusion of hands and heads, and something waved. I saw it, just in time to signal the driver, Stop! He shut off, and put his brake on, but the train drifted past here a hundred and fifty yards or more. I ran after it, and, as I went along, heard terrible screams and cries. A beautiful young lady had died instantaneously in one of the compartments, and was brought in here, and laid down on this floor between us.'

Involuntarily, I pushed my chair back, as I looked from the boards at which he pointed, to himself.

'True, sir. True. Precisely as it happened, so I tell it you.'

I could think of nothing to say, to any purpose, and my mouth was very dry. The wind and the wires took up the story with a long lamenting wail.

He resumed. 'Now, sir, mark this, and judge how my mind is troubled. The spectre came back, a week ago. Ever since, it has been there, now and again, by fits and starts.'

'At the light?'

'At the Danger-light.'

'What does it seem to do?'

He repeated, if possible with increased passion and vehemence, that former gesticulation of 'For God's sake clear the way!'

Then, he went on. 'I have no peace or rest for it. It calls to me, for many minutes together, in an agonised manner, 'Below there! Look out! Look out!' It stands waving to me. It rings my little bell——'

I caught at that. 'Did it ring your bell yesterday evening when I was here, and you went to the door?'

'Twice.'

'Why, see,' said I, 'how your imagination misleads you. My eyes were on the bell, and my ears were open to the bell, and if I am a living man, it did NOT ring at those times. No, nor at any other time, except when it was rung in the natural course of physical things by the station communicating with you.'

He shook his head. 'I have never made a mistake as to that, yet, sir. I have never confused the spectre's ring with the man's. The ghost's ring is a strange vibration in the bell that it derives from nothing else, and I have not asserted that the bell stirs to the eye. I don't wonder that you failed to hear it. But I heard it.'

'And did the spectre seem to be there, when you looked out?'

'It WAS there.'

'Both times?'

He repeated firmly: 'Both times.'

'Will you come to the door with me, and look for it now?'

He bit his under-lip as though he were somewhat unwilling, but arose. I opened the door, and stood on the step, while he stood in the doorway. There, was the Danger-light. There, was the dismal mouth of the tunnel. There, were the high wet stone walls of the cutting. There, were the stars above them.

'Do you see it?' I asked him, taking particular note of his face. His eyes were prominent and strained; but not very much more so, perhaps, than my own had been when I had directed them earnestly towards the same spot.

'No,' he answered. 'It is not there.'

'Agreed,' said I.

We went in again, shut the door, and resumed our seats. I was thinking how best to improve this advantage, if it might be called one, when he took up the conversation in such a matter of course way, so assuming that there could be no serious question of fact between us, that I felt myself placed in the weakest of positions.

'By this time you will fully understand, sir,' he said, 'that what troubles me so dreadfully, is the question; what does the spectre mean?'

I was not sure, I told him, that I did fully understand.

'What is it warning against?' he said, ruminating, with his eyes on the fire, and only by times turning them on me. 'What is the danger? Where is the danger? There is danger overhanging, somewhere on the Line. Some dreadful calamity will happen. It is not to be doubted this third time, after what has gone before. But surely this is a cruel haunting of me. What can I do?'

He pulled out his handkerchief, and wiped the drops from his heated forehead.

'If I telegraph Danger, on either side of me, or on both, I can give no reason for it,' he went on, wiping the palms of his hands. 'I should get into trouble, and do no good. They would think I was mad. This is the way it would work: Message: 'Danger! Take care!' Answer: 'What danger? Where?' Message: 'Don't know. But for God's sake take care!' They would displace me. What else could they do?'

His pain of mind was most pitiable to see. It was the mental torture of a conscientious man, oppressed beyond endurance by an unintelligible responsibility involving life.

'When it first stood under the Danger-light,' he went on, putting his dark hair back from his head, and drawing his hands outward across and across his temples in an extremity of feverish distress, 'Why not tell me where that accident was to happen—if it must happen? Why not tell me how it could be averted—if it could have been averted? When on its second coming it hid its face, why not tell me instead; 'She is going to die. Let them keep her at home?' If it came, on those two occasions, only to show me that its warnings were true, and so to prepare me for the third, why not warn me plainly now? And I, Lord help me! A mere poor signalman on this solitary station! Why not go to somebody with credit to be believed, and power to act!'

When I saw him in this state, I saw that for the poor man's sake, as well as for the public safety, what I had to do for the time was, to compose his mind. Therefore, setting aside all question of reality or unreality between us, I represented to him that whoever thoroughly discharged his duty, must do well, and that at least it was his comfort that he understood his duty, though he did not understand these confounding appearances. In this effort I succeeded far better than in the attempt to reason him out of his conviction. He became calm; the occupations incidental to his post as the night advanced, began to make larger demands on his attention; and I left him at two in the morning. I had offered to stay through the night, but he would not hear of it.

That I more than once looked back at the red light as I ascended the pathway, that I did not like the red light, and that I should have slept but poorly if my bed had been under it, I see no reason to conceal. Nor, did I like the two sequences of the accident and the dead girl. I see no reason to conceal that, either.

But, what ran most in my thoughts was the consideration how ought I to act, having become the recipient of this disclosure? I had proved the man to be intelligent, vigilant, painstaking, and exact; but how long might he remain so, in his state of mind? Though in a subordinate position, still he held a most important trust, and would I (for instance) like to stake my own life on the chances of his continuing to execute it with precision?

Unable to overcome a feeling that there would be something treacherous in my communicating what he had told me, to his superiors in the Company, without first being plain with himself and proposing a middle course to him, I ultimately resolved to offer to accompany him (otherwise keeping his secret for the present) to the wisest medical practitioner we could hear of in those parts, and to take his opinion. A change in his time of duty would come round next night, he had apprised me, and he would be off an hour or two after sunrise, and on again soon after sunset. I had appointed to return accordingly.

Next evening was a lovely evening, and I walked out early to enjoy it. The sun was not yet quite down when I traversed the field-path near the top of the deep cutting. I would extend my walk for an hour, I said to myself, half an hour on and half an hour back, and it would then be time to go to my signalman's box.

Before pursuing my stroll, I stepped to the brink, and mechanically looked down, from the point from which I had first seen him. I cannot describe the thrill that seized upon me, when, close at the mouth of the tunnel, I saw the appearance of a man, with his left sleeve across his eyes, passionately waving his right arm.

The nameless horror that oppressed me, passed in a moment, for in a moment I saw that this appearance of a man was a man indeed, and that there was a little group of other men standing at a short distance, to whom he seemed to be rehearsing the gesture he made. The Danger-light was not yet lighted. Against its shaft, a little low hut, entirely new to me, had been made of some wooden supports and tarpaulin. It looked no bigger than a bed.

With an irresistible sense that something was wrong—with a flashing self-reproachful fear that fatal mischief had come of my leaving the man there, and causing no one to be sent to overlook or correct what he did—I descended the notched path with all the speed I could make.

'What is the matter?' I asked the men.

'Signalman killed this morning, sir.'

'Not the man belonging to that box?'

'Yes, sir.'

'Not the man I know?'

'You will recognise him, sir, if you knew him,' said the man who spoke for the others, solemnly uncovering his own head and raising an end of the tarpaulin, 'for his face is quite composed.'

'O! How did this happen, how did this happen?' I asked, turning from one to another as the hut closed in again.

'He was cut down by an engine, sir. No man in England knew his work better. But somehow he was not clear of the outer rail.

It was just at broad day. He had struck the light, and had the lamp in his hand. As the engine came out of the tunnel, his back was towards her, and she cut him down. That man drove her, and was showing how it happened. Show the gentleman, Tom.'

The man, who wore a rough dark dress, stepped back to his former place at the mouth of the tunnel!

'Coming round the curve in the tunnel, sir,' he said, 'I saw him at the end, like as if I saw him down a perspective glass. There was no time to check speed, and I knew him to be very careful. As he didn't seem to take heed of the whistle, I shut it off when we were running down upon him, and called to him as loud as I could call.'

'What did you say?'

'I said, Below there! Look out! Look out! For God's sake clear the way!'

I started.

'Ah! it was a dreadful time, sir. I never left off calling to him. I put this arm before my eyes, not to see, and I waved this arm to the last; but it was no use.'

Without prolonging the narrative to dwell on any one of its curious circumstances more than on any other, I may, in closing it, point out the coincidence that the warning of the engine driver included, not only the words which the unfortunate Signalman had repeated to me as haunting him, but also the words which I myself—not he—had attached, and that only in my own mind, to the gesticulation he had imitated.

3

THE TRIAL FOR MURDER

I have always noticed a prevalent want of courage, even among persons of superior intelligence and culture, as to imparting their own psychological experiences when those have been of a strange sort. Almost all men are afraid that what they could relate in such wise would find no parallel or response in a listener's internal life, and might be suspected or laughed at. A truthful traveller, who should have seen some extraordinary creature in the likeness of a sea serpent, would have no fear of mentioning it; but the same traveller, having had some singular presentiment, impulse, vagary of thought, vision (so-called), dream, or other remarkable mental impression, would hesitate considerably before he would own to it. To this reticence, I attribute much of the obscurity in which such subjects are involved. We do not habitually communicate our experiences of these subjective things as we do our experiences of objective creation. The consequence is, that the general stock of experience in this regard appears exceptional, and really is so, in respect of being miserably imperfect.

In what way I am going to relate, I have no intention of setting up, opposing, or supporting, any theory whatever. I know the history of the Bookseller of Berlin, I have studied the case of the wife of a late Astronomer Royal as related by Sir David Brewster, and I have followed the minutest details of a much more remarkable case of Spectral Illusion occurring within my private circle of friends. It may be necessary to state as to this last, that the sufferer (a lady) was in no degree, however distant, related to me. A mistaken assumption on that head might suggest an explanation of a part of my own case but only a part which would be wholly without foundation. It cannot be referred to my inheritance of any developed peculiarity, nor had I ever before any at all similar experience, nor have I ever had any at all similar experience since.

It does not signify how many years ago, or how few, a certain murder was committed in England, which attracted great attention. We hear more than enough of murderers as they rise in succession to their atrocious eminence, and I would bury the memory of this particular brute, if I could, as his body was buried, in Newgate Jail. I purposely abstain from giving any direct clue to the criminal's individuality.

When the murder was first discovered, no suspicion fell—or I ought rather to say, for I cannot be too precise in my facts, it was nowhere publicly hinted that any suspicion fell—on the man who was afterwards brought to trial. As no reference was at that time made to him in the newspapers, it is obviously impossible that any description of him can at that time have been given in the newspapers. It is essential that this fact be remembered.

Unfolding at breakfast my morning paper, containing the account of that first discovery, I found it to be deeply interesting, and I read it with close attention. I read it twice, if not three times. The discovery had been made in a bedroom, and, when I laid down the paper, I was aware of a flash—rush—flow—I do not know what to call it—no word I can find is satisfactorily descriptive—in which I seemed to see that bedroom passing through my room, like a picture impossibly painted on a running river. Though almost instantaneous in its passing, it was perfectly clear; so clear that I distinctly, and with a sense of relief, observed the absence of the dead body from the bed.

It was in no romantic place that I had this curious sensation, but in chambers in Piccadilly, very near to the corner of St. James's Street. It was entirely new to me. I was in my easy chair at the moment, and the sensation was accompanied with a peculiar shiver which started the chair from its position. (But it is to be noted that the chair ran easily on castors.) I went to one of the windows (there are two in the room, and the room is on the second floor) to refresh my eyes with the moving objects down in Piccadilly. It was a bright autumn morning, and the street was sparkling and cheerful. The wind was high. As I looked out, it brought down from the park a quantity of fallen leaves, which a gust took, and whirled into a spiral pillar. As the pillar fell and the leaves dispersed, I saw two men on the opposite side of the way, going from West to East. They were one behind the other. The foremost man often looked back over his shoulder. The second man followed him, at a distance of some thirty paces, with his right hand menacingly raised. First, the singularity and steadiness of this threatening gesture in so public a thoroughfare attracted my attention; and next, the more remarkable circumstance that nobody heeded it. Both men threaded their way among the other passengers with a smoothness hardly consistent even with the action of walking on a pavement; and no single creature, that I could see, gave them place, touched them, or looked after them. In passing before my windows, they both stared up at me. I saw their two faces very distinctly, and I knew that I could recognise them anywhere. Not that I had consciously noticed anything very remarkable in either face, except that the man who went first had an unusually lowering appearance, and that the face of the man who followed him was of the colour of impure wax.

I am a bachelor, and my valet and his wife constitute my whole establishment. My occupation is in a certain Branch Bank, and I wish that my duties as head of a Department were as light as they are popularly supposed to be. They kept me in town that autumn, when I stood in need of change. I was not ill, but I was not well. My reader is to make the most that can be reasonably made of my feeling jaded, having a depressing sense upon me of a monotonous life, and being 'slightly dyspeptic'. I am assured by my renowned doctor that my real state of health at that time justifies no stronger description, and I quote his own from his written answer to my request for it.

As the circumstances of the murder, gradually unravelling, took stronger and stronger possession of the public mind, I kept them away from mine by knowing as little about them as was possible in the midst of the universal excitement. But I knew that a verdict of Wilful Murder had been found against the suspected murderer, and that he had been committed to Newgate for trial. I also knew that his trial had been postponed over one sessions of the Central Criminal Court, on the ground of general prejudice and want of time for the preparation of the defence. I may further have known, but I believe I did not, when, or about when, the Sessions to which his trial stood postponed would come on.

My sitting room, bedroom, and dressing room, are all on one floor. With the last there is no communication but through the bedroom. True, there is a door in it, once communicating with the staircase; but a part of the fitting of my bath has been—and had then been for some years—fixed across it. At the same period, and as a part of the same arrangement—the door had been nailed up and canvased over.

I was standing in my bedroom late one night, giving some directions to my servant before he went to bed. My face was towards the only available door of communication with the dressing room, and it was closed. My servant's back was towards that door. While I was speaking to him, I saw it open, and a man look in, who very earnestly and mysteriously beckoned to me. That man was the man who had gone second of the two along Piccadilly, and whose face was of the colour of impure wax.

The figure, having beckoned, drew back, and closed the door. With no longer pause than was made by my crossing the bedroom, I opened the dressing room door, and looked in. I had a lighted candle already in my hand. I felt no inward expectation of seeing the figure in the dressing room, and I did not see it there.

Conscious that my servant stood amazed, I turned round to him, and said: 'Derrick, could you believe that in my cool senses I fancied I saw a—'. As I there laid my hand upon his breast, with a sudden start he trembled violently, and said, 'O Lord, yes, sir! A dead man beckoning!'

Now I do not believe that this John Derrick, my trusty and attached servant for more than twenty years, had any impression whatever of having seen any such figure, until I touched him. The change in him was so startling, when I touched him, that I fully believe he derived his impression in some occult manner from me at that instant.

I bade John Derrick to bring some brandy, and I gave him a dram, and was glad to take one myself. Of what had preceded that night's phenomenon, I told him not a single word. Reflecting on it, I was absolutely certain that I had never seen that face before, except on the one occasion in Piccadilly. Comparing its expression when beckoning at the door with its expression when it had stared up at me as I stood at my window, I came to the conclusion that on the first occasion it had sought to fasten itself upon my memory, and that on the second occasion it had made sure of being immediately remembered.

I was not very comfortable that night, though I felt a certainty, difficult to explain, that the figure would not return. At daylight I fell into a heavy sleep, from which I was awakened by John Derrick's coming to my bedside with a paper in his hand.

This paper, it appeared, had been the subject of an altercation at the door between its bearer and my servant. It was a summons to me to serve upon a Jury at the forthcoming Sessions of the

Central Criminal Court at the Old Bailey. I had never before been summoned on such a Jury, as John Derrick well knew. He believed—I am not certain at this hour whether with reason or otherwise—that that class of Jurors were customarily chosen on a lower qualification than mine, and he had at first refused to accept the summons. The man who served it had taken the matter very coolly. He had said that my attendance or non-attendance was nothing to him; there the summons was; and I should deal with it at my own peril, and not at his.

For a day or two, I was undecided whether to respond to this call, or take no notice of it. I was not conscious of the slightest mysterious bias, influence, or attraction, one way or other. Of that I am as strictly sure as of every other statement that I make here. Ultimately I decided, as a break in the monotony of my life, that I would go.

The appointed morning was a raw morning in the month of November. There was a dense brown fog in Piccadilly, and it became positively black and in the last degree oppressive East of Temple Bar. I found the passages and staircases of the Court-House flaringly lighted with gas, and the Court itself similarly illuminated. I think that, until I was conducted by officers into the Old Court and saw its crowded state, I did not know that the Murderer was to be tried that day. I think that, until I was so helped into the Old Court with considerable difficulty, I did not know into which of the two Courts sitting my summons would take me. But this must not be received as a positive assertion, for I am not completely satisfied in my mind on either point.

I took my seat in the place appropriated to Jurors in waiting, and I looked about the Court as well as I could through the cloud of fog and breath that was heavy in it. I noticed the black vapour hanging like a murky curtain outside the great windows, and I noticed the stifled sound of wheels on the straw or tan that was littered in the street; also, the hum of the people gathered there, which a shrill whistle, or a louder song or hail than the rest, occasionally pierced. Soon afterwards the Judges, two in number, entered, and took their seats. The buzz in the Court was awfully hushed. The direction was given to put the Murderer to the bar. He appeared there. And in that same instant I recognised in him the first of the two men who had gone down Piccadilly.

If my name had been called then, I doubt if I could have answered to it audibly. But it was called about sixth or eighth in the panel, and I was by that time able to say, 'Here!' Now, observe. As I stepped into the box, the prisoner, who had been looking on attentively, but with no sign of concern, became violently agitated, and beckoned to his attorney. The prisoner's wish to challenge me was so manifest, that it occasioned a pause, during which the attorney, with his hand upon the dock, whispered with his client, and shook his head. I afterwards had it from that gentleman, that the prisoner's first affrighted words to him were, 'At all hazards, challenge that man!' But that, as he would give no reason for it, and admitted that he had not even known my name until he heard it called and I appeared, it was not done.

Both on the ground already explained, that I wish to avoid reviving the unwholesome memory of that Murderer, and also because a detailed account of his long trial is by no means indispensable to my narrative, I shall confine myself closely to such incidents in the ten days and nights during which we, the Jury, were kept together, as directly bear on my own curious personal experience. It is in that, and not in the Murderer, that I seek to interest my reader. It is to that, and not to a page of the Newgate Calendar, that I beg attention.

I was chosen Foreman of the Jury. On the second morning of the trial, after evidence had been taken for two hours (I heard the church clocks strike), happening to cast my eyes over my brother jurymen, I found an inexplicable difficulty in counting them. I counted them several times, yet always with the same difficulty.

In short, I made them one too many.

I touched the brother jurymen whose place was next me, and I whispered to him, 'Oblige me by counting us.' He looked surprised by the request, but turned his head and counted. 'Why,' says he, suddenly, 'we are Thirt—; but no, it's not possible. No. We are twelve.'

According to my counting that day, we were always right in detail, but in the gross we were always one too many. There was no appearance—no figure—to account for it; but I had now an inward foreshadowing of the figure that was surely coming.

The Jury were housed at the London Tavern. We all slept in one large room on separate tables, and we were constantly in the charge and under the eye of the officer sworn to hold us in safe-keeping. I see no reason for suppressing the real name of that officer. He was intelligent, highly polite, and obliging, and (I was glad to hear) much respected in the City. He had an agreeable presence, good eyes, enviable black whiskers, and a fine sonorous voice. His name was Mr Harker.

When we turned into our twelve beds at night, Mr Harker's bed was drawn across the door. On the night of the second day, not being disposed to lie down, and seeing Mr Harker sitting on his bed, I went and sat beside him, and offered him a pinch of snuff. As Mr Harker's hand touched mine in taking it from my box, a peculiar shiver crossed him, and he said, 'Who is this?'

Following Mr Harker's eyes, and looking along the room, I saw again the figure I expected,—the second of the two men who had gone down Piccadilly. I rose, and advanced a few steps; then stopped, and looked round at Mr Harker. He was quite unconcerned, laughed, and said in a pleasant way, 'I thought for a moment we had a thirteenth juryman, without a bed. But I see it is the moonlight.'

Making no revelation to Mr Harker, but inviting him to take a walk with me to the end of the room, I watched what the figure did. It stood for a few moments by the bedside of each of my eleven brother jurymen, close to the pillow. It always went to the right-hand side of the bed, and always passed out crossing the foot of the next bed. It seemed, from the action of the head, merely to look down pensively at each recumbent figure. It took no notice of me, or of my bed, which was that nearest to Mr Harker's. It seemed to go out where the moonlight came in, through a high window, as by an aerial flight of stairs.

Next morning at breakfast, it appeared that everybody present had dreamed of the murdered man last night, except myself and Mr Harker.

I now felt as convinced that the second man who had gone down Piccadilly was the murdered man (so to speak), as if it had been borne into my comprehension by his immediate testimony. But even this took place, and in a manner for which I was not at all prepared.

On the fifth day of the trial, when the case for the prosecution was drawing to a close, a miniature of the murdered man, missing from his bedroom upon the discovery of the deed, and afterwards found in a hiding place where the Murderer had been seen digging, was put in evidence. Having been identified by the witness under examination, it was handed up to the Bench, and thence handed down to be inspected by the Jury. As an officer in a black gown was making his way with it across to me, the figure of the second man who had gone down Piccadilly impetuously started from the crowd, caught the miniature from the officer, and gave it to me with his own hands, at the same time saying, in a low and hollow tone,—before I saw the miniature, which was in a locket,—' I was younger then, and my face was not then drained of blood.' It also came between me and the brother juryman to whom I would have given the miniature, and between him and the brother juryman to whom he would have given it, and so passed it on through the whole of our number, and back into my possession. Not one of them, however, detected this.

At table, and generally when we were shut up together in Mr Harker's custody, we had from the first naturally discussed the day's proceedings a good deal. On that fifth day, the case for the prosecution being closed, and we having that side of the question in a completed shape before us, our discussion was more animated and serious. Among our number was a vestryman,—the densest idiot I have ever seen at large,—who met the plainest evidence with the most preposterous objections, and who was sided with by two flabby parochial parasites; all the three impanelled from a district so delivered over to Fever that they ought to have been upon their own trial for five hundred Murders. When these mischievous blockheads were at their loudest, which was towards midnight, while some of us were already preparing for bed, I again saw the murdered man. He stood grimly behind them, beckoning to me. On my going towards them, and striking into the conversation, he immediately retired. This was the beginning of a separate series of appearances, confined to that long room in which we were confined. Whenever a knot of my brother jurymen laid their heads together, I saw the head of the murdered man among theirs. Whenever their comparison of notes was going against him, he would solemnly and irresistibly beckon to me.

It will be borne in mind that down to the production of the miniature, on the fifth day of the trial, I had never seen the Appearance in Court. Three changes occurred now that we entered on the case for the defence. Two of them I will mention together, first. The figure was now in Court continually, and it never there addressed itself to me, but always to the person who was speaking at the time. For instance: the throat of the murdered man had been cut straight across. In the opening speech for the defence, it was suggested that the deceased might have cut his own throat. At that very moment, the figure, with its throat in the dreadful condition referred to (this it had concealed before), stood at the speaker's elbow, motioning across and across its windpipe, now with the right hand, now with the left, vigorously suggesting to the speaker himself the impossibility of such a wound having been self-inflicted by either hand. For another instance: a witness to character, a woman, deposed to the prisoner's being the most amiable of mankind. The figure at that instant stood on the floor before her, looking her full in the face, and pointing out the prisoner's evil countenance with an extended arm and an outstretched finger.

The third change now to be added impressed me strongly as the most marked and striking of all. I do not theorise upon it; I accurately state it, and there leave it. Although the Appearance was not itself perceived by those whom it addressed, its coming close to such persons was invariably attended by some trepidation or disturbance on their part. It seemed to me as if it were prevented, by laws to which I was not amenable, from fully revealing itself to others, and yet as if it could invisibly, dumbly, and darkly overshadow their minds. When the leading counsel for the defence suggested that hypothesis of suicide, and the figure stood at the learned gentleman's elbow, frightfully sawing at its severed throat, it is undeniable that the counsel faltered in his speech, lost for a few seconds the thread of his ingenious discourse, wiped his forehead with his handkerchief, and turned extremely pale. When the witness to character was confronted by the Appearance, her eyes most certainly did follow the direction of its pointed finger, and rest in great hesitation and trouble upon the prisoner's face. Two additional illustrations will suffice. On the eighth day of the trial, after the pause which was every day made early in the afternoon for a few minutes' rest and refreshment, I came back into Court with the rest of the Jury some little time before the return of the Judges. Standing up in the box and looking about me, I thought the figure was not there, until, chancing to raise my eyes to the gallery, I saw it bending forward, and leaning over a very decent woman, as if to assure itself whether the Judges had resumed their seats or not. Immediately afterwards that woman screamed, fainted, and was carried out. So with the venerable, sagacious, and patient Judge who conducted the trial. When the case was over, and he settled himself and his papers to sum up, the murdered man, entering by the Judges' door, advanced to his Lordship's desk, and looked eagerly over his shoulder at the pages of his notes which he was turning. A change came over his Lordship's face; his hand stopped; the peculiar shiver, that I knew so well, passed over him; he faltered, 'Excuse me, gentlemen, for a few moments. I am somewhat oppressed by the vitiated air.' and did not recover until he had drunk a glass of water.

Through all the monotony of six of those interminable ten days,—the same Judges and others on the bench, the same Murderer in the dock, the same lawyers at the table, the same tones of question and answer rising to the roof of the court, the same scratching of the Judge's pen, the same ushers going in and out, the same lights kindled at the same hour when there had been any natural light of day, the same foggy curtain outside the great windows when it was foggy, the same rain pattering and dripping when it was rainy, the same footmarks of turnkeys and prisoner day after day on the same sawdust, the same keys locking and unlocking the same heavy doors,—through all the wearisome monotony which made me feel as if I had been Foreman of the Jury for a vast period of time, and Piccadilly had flourished coevally with Babylon, the murdered man never lost one trace of his distinctness in my eyes, nor was he at any moment less distinct than anybody else. I must not omit, as a matter of fact, that I never once saw the Appearance which I call by the name of the murdered man look at the Murderer. Again and again I wondered, 'Why does he not?' But he never did.

Nor did he look at me, after the production of the miniature, until the last closing minutes of the trial arrived. We retired to consider, at seven minutes before ten at night. The idiotic vestryman and his two parochial parasites gave us so much trouble that we twice returned into Court to beg to have certain extracts from the Judge's notes re-read. Nine of us had not the smallest doubt about those passages, neither, I believe, had any one in the Court; the dunder-headed triumvirate, having no idea but obstruction, disputed them for that very reason. At length we prevailed, and finally the Jury returned into Court at ten minutes past twelve.

The murdered man at that time stood directly opposite the Jury-box, on the other side of the Court. As I took my place, his eyes rested on me with great attention; he seemed satisfied, and slowly shook a great gray veil, which he carried on his arm for the first time, over his head and whole form. As I gave in our verdict, 'Guilty,' the veil collapsed, all was gone, and his place was empty.

The Murderer, being asked by the Judge, according to usage, whether he had anything to say before sentence of Death should be passed upon him, indistinctly muttered something which was described in the leading newspapers of the following day as 'a few rambling, incoherent, and half-audible words, in which he was understood to complain that he had not had a fair trial, because the Foreman of the Jury was prepossessed against him.' The remarkable declaration that he really made was this: 'My Lord, I knew I was a doomed man when the Foreman of my Jury came into the box. My Lord I knew he would never let me off because before I was taken he somehow got to my bedside in the night woke me and put a rope round my neck.'

4

HUNTED DOWN

Most of us see some romances in life. In my capacity as Chief Manager of a Life Assurance Office, I think, I have within the last thirty years seen more romances than the generality of men, however unpromising the opportunity may, at first sight, seem.

As I have retired, and live at my ease, I possess the means that I used to want, of considering what I have seen, at leisure. My experiences have a more remarkable aspect, so reviewed, than they had when they were in progress. I have come home from the play now, and can recall the scenes of the Drama upon which the curtain has fallen, free from the glare, bewilderment, and bustle of the Theatre.

Let me recall one of these Romances of the real world.

There is nothing truer than physiognomy, taken in connection with manner. The art of reading that book of which Eternal Wisdom obliges every human creature to present his or her own page with the individual character written on it, is a difficult one, perhaps, and is little studied. It may require some natural aptitude, and it must require (for everything does) some patience and some pains. That these are not usually given to it,—that numbers of people accept a few stock commonplace expressions of the face as the whole list of characteristics, and neither seek nor know the refinements that are truest,—that You, for instance, give a great deal of time and attention to the reading of music, Greek, Latin, French, Italian, Hebrew, if you please, and do not qualify yourself to read the face of the master or mistress looking over your shoulder teaching it to you,—I assume to be five hundred times more probable than improbable. Perhaps a little self-sufficiency may be at the bottom of this; facial expression requires no study from you, you think; it comes by nature to you to know enough about it, and you are not to be taken in.

I confess, for my part, that I have been taken in, over and over again. I have been taken in by acquaintances, and I have been taken in (of course) by friends; far oftener by friends than by any other class of persons. How came I to be so deceived? Had I quite misread their faces?

No. Believe me, my first impression of those people, founded on face and manner alone, was invariably true. My mistake was in suffering them to come nearer to me and explain themselves away.

The partition which separated my own office from our general outer office in the City was of thick plate-glass. I could see through it what passed in the outer office, without hearing a word. I had it put up in place of a wall that had been there for years,—ever since the house was built. It is no matter whether I did or did not make the change in order that I might derive my first impression of strangers, who came to us on business, from their faces alone, without being influenced by anything they said. Enough to mention that I turned my glass partition to that account, and that a Life Assurance Office is at all times exposed to be practised upon by the most crafty and cruel of the human race.

It was through my glass partition that I first saw the gentleman whose story I am going to tell.

He had come in without my observing it, and had put his hat and umbrella on the broad counter, and was bending over it to take some papers from one of the clerks.

He was about forty or so, dark, exceedingly well dressed in black,—being in mourning,—and the hand he extended with a polite air, had a particularly well-fitting black-kid glove upon it. His hair, which was elaborately brushed and oiled, was parted straight up the middle; and he presented this parting to the clerk, exactly (to my thinking) as if he had said, in so many words: 'You must take me, if you please, my friend, just as I show myself. Come straight up here, follow the gravel path, keep off the grass, I allow no trespassing.'

I conceived a very great aversion to that man the moment I thus saw him.

He had asked for some of our printed forms, and the clerk was giving them to him and explaining them. An obliged and agreeable smile was on his face, and his eyes met those of the clerk with a sprightly look. (I have known a vast quantity of nonsense talked about bad men not looking you in the face. Don't trust that conventional idea. Dishonesty will stare honesty out of countenance, any day in the week, if there is anything to be got by it.)

I saw, in the corner of his eyelash, that he became aware of my looking at him. Immediately he turned the parting in his hair toward the glass partition, as if he said to me with a sweet smile, 'Straight up here, if you please. Off the grass!'

In a few moments he had put on his hat and taken up his umbrella, and was gone.

I beckoned the clerk into my room, and asked, 'Who was that?'

He had the gentleman's card in his hand. 'Mr Julius Slinkton, Middle Temple.'

'A barrister, Mr Adams?'

'I think not, sir.'

'I should have thought him a clergyman, but for his having no Reverend here,' said I.

'Probably, from his appearance,' Mr Adams replied, 'he is reading for orders.'

I should mention that he wore a dainty white cravat, and dainty linen altogether.

'What did he want, Mr Adams?'

'Merely a form of proposal, sir, and form of reference.'

'Recommended here? Did he say?'

'Yes, he said he was recommended here by a friend of yours. He noticed you, but said that as he had not the pleasure of your personal acquaintance he would not trouble you.'

'Did he know my name?'

'O yes, sir! He said, "There is Mr Sampson, I see!"'

'A well-spoken gentleman, apparently?'

'Remarkably so, sir.'

'Insinuating manners, apparently?'

'Very much so, indeed, sir.'

'Hah!' said I. 'I want nothing at present, Mr Adams.'

Within a fortnight of that day I went to dine with a friend of mine, a merchant, a man of taste, who buys pictures and books, and the first man I saw among the company was Mr Julius Slinkton. There he was, standing before the fire, with good large eyes and an open expression of face; but still (I thought) requiring everybody to come at him by the prepared way he offered, and by no other.

I noticed him ask my friend to introduce him to Mr Sampson, and my friend did so. Mr Slinkton was very happy to see me. Not too happy; there was no over-doing of the matter; happy in a thoroughly well-bred, perfectly unmeaning way.

'I thought you had met,' our host observed.

'No,' said Mr Slinkton. 'I did look in at Mr Sampson's office, on your recommendation; but I really did not feel justified in troubling Mr Sampson himself, on a point in the everyday, routine of an ordinary clerk.'

I said I should have been glad to show him any attention on

our friend's introduction.

'I am sure of that,' said he, 'and am much obliged. At another time, perhaps, I may be less delicate. Only, however, if I have real business; for I know, Mr Sampson, how precious business time is, and what a vast number of impertinent people there are in the world.'

I acknowledged his consideration with a slight bow. 'You were thinking,' said I, 'of effecting a policy on your life.'

'O dear no! I am afraid I am not so prudent as you pay me the compliment of supposing me to be, Mr Sampson. I merely inquired for a friend. But you know what friends are in such matters. Nothing may ever come of it. I have the greatest reluctance to trouble men of business with inquiries for friends, knowing the probabilities to be a thousand to one that the friends will never follow them up. People are so fickle, so selfish, so inconsiderate. Don't you, in your business, find them so every day, Mr Sampson?'

I was going to give a qualified answer; but he turned his smooth, white parting on me with its 'Straight up here, if you please!' and I answered 'Yes.'

'I hear, Mr Sampson,' he resumed presently, for our friend had a new cook, and dinner was not so punctual as usual, 'that your profession has recently suffered a great loss.'

'In money?' said I.

He laughed at my ready association of loss with money, and replied, 'No, in talent and vigour.'

Not at once following out his allusion, I considered for a moment. 'Has it sustained a loss of that kind?' said I. 'I was not aware of it.'

'Understand me, Mr Sampson. I don't imagine that you have retired. It is not so bad as that. But Mr Meltham—'

'O, to be sure!' said I. 'Yes! Mr Meltham, the young actuary of the 'Inestimable.''

'Just so,' he returned in a consoling way.

'He is a great loss. He was at once the most profound, the most original, and the most energetic man I have ever known connected with Life Assurance.'

I spoke strongly; for I had a high esteem and admiration for Meltham; and my gentleman had indefinitely conveyed to me some suspicion that he wanted to sneer at him. He recalled me to my guard by presenting that trim pathway up his head, with its internal 'Not on the grass, if you please—the gravel.'

'You knew him, Mr Slinkton.'

'Only by reputation. To have known him as an acquaintance or as a friend, is an honour I should have sought if he had remained in society, though I might never have had the good fortune to attain it, being a man of far inferior mark. He was scarcely above thirty, I suppose?'

'About thirty.'

'Ah!' he sighed in his former consoling way. 'What creatures we are! To break up, Mr Sampson, and become incapable of business at that time of life!—Any reason assigned for the melancholy fact?'

('Humph!' thought I, as I looked at him. 'But I won't go up the track, and I will go on the grass.')

'What reason have you heard assigned, Mr Slinkton?' I asked, point-blank.

'Most likely a false one. You know what Rumour is, Mr Sampson. I never repeat what I hear; it is the only way of paring the nails and shaving the head of Rumour. But when you ask me what reason I have heard assigned for Mr Meltham's passing away from among men, it is another thing. I am not gratifying idle gossip then.

I was told, Mr Sampson, that Mr Meltham had relinquished all his avocations and all his prospects, because he was, in fact, broken- hearted. A disappointed attachment I heard,—though it hardly seems probable, in the case of a man so distinguished and so attractive.'

'Attractions and distinctions are no armour against death,' said I.

'O, she died? Pray pardon me. I did not hear that. That, indeed, makes it very, very sad. Poor Mr Meltham! She died? Ah, dear me! Lamentable, lamentable!'

I still thought his pity was not quite genuine, and I still suspected an unaccountable sneer under all this, until he said, as we were parted, like the other knots of talkers, by the announcement of dinner:

'Mr Sampson, you are surprised to see me so moved on behalf of a man whom I have never known. I am not so disinterested as you may suppose. I have suffered, and recently too, from death myself. I have lost one of two charming nieces, who were my constant companions. She died young—barely three-and-twenty; and even her remaining sister is far from strong. The world is a grave!'

He said this with deep feeling, and I felt reproached for the coldness of my manner. Coldness and distrust had been engendered in me, I knew, by my bad experiences; they were not natural to me; and I often thought how much I had lost in life, losing trustfulness, and how little I had gained, gaining hard caution. This state of mind being habitual to me, I troubled myself more about this conversation than I might have troubled myself about a greater matter. I listened to his talk at dinner, and observed how readily other men responded to it, and with what a graceful instinct he adapted his subjects to the knowledge and habits of those he talked with. As, in talking with me, he had easily started the subject I might be supposed to understand best, and to be the most interested in, so, in talking with others, he guided himself by the same rule. The company was of a varied character; but he was not at fault, that I could discover, with any member of it. He knew just as much of each man's pursuit as made him agreeable to that man in reference to it, and just as little as made it natural in him to seek modestly for information when the theme was broached.

As he talked and talked—but really not too much, for the rest of us seemed to force it upon him—I became quite angry with myself. I took his face to pieces in my mind, like a watch, and examined it in detail. I could not say much against any of his features separately; I could say even less against them when they were put together. 'Then is it not monstrous,' I asked myself, 'that because a man happens to part his hair straight up the middle of his head, I should permit myself to suspect, and even to detest him?'

(I may stop to remark that this was no proof of my sense. An observer of men who finds himself steadily repelled by some apparently trifling thing in a stranger is right to give it great weight. It may be the clue to the whole mystery. A hair or two will show where a lion is hidden. A very little key will open a very heavy door.)

I took my part in the conversation with him after a time, and we got on remarkably well. In the drawing-room I asked the host how long he had known Mr Slinkton.

He answered, not many months; he had met him at the house of a celebrated painter then present, who had known him well when he was travelling with his nieces in Italy for their health. His plans in life being broken by the death of one of them, he was reading with the intention of going back to college as a matter of form, taking his degree, and going into orders. I could not but argue with myself that here was the true explanation of his interest in poor Meltham, and that I had been almost brutal in my distrust on that simple head.

On the very next day but one I was sitting behind my glass partition, as before, when he came into the outer office, as before. The moment I saw him again without hearing him, I hated him worse than ever.

It was only for a moment that I had this opportunity; for he waved his tight-fitting black glove the instant I looked at him, and came straight in.

'Mr Sampson, good-day! I presume, you see, upon your kind permission to intrude upon you. I don't keep my word in being justified by business, for my business here—if I may so abuse the word—is of the slightest nature.'

I asked, was it anything I could assist him in?

'I thank you, no. I merely called to inquire outside whether my dilatory friend had been so false to himself as to be practical and sensible. But, of course, he has done nothing. I gave him your papers with my own hand, and he was hot upon the intention, but of course he has done nothing. Apart from the general human disinclination to do anything that ought to be done, I dare say there is a specially about assuring one's life. You find it like will-making. People are so superstitious, and take it for granted they will die soon afterwards.'

'Up here, if you please; straight up here, Mr Sampson. Neither to the right nor to the left.' I almost fancied I could hear him breathe the words as he sat smiling at me, with that intolerable parting exactly opposite the bridge of my nose.

'There is such a feeling sometimes, no doubt,' I replied; 'but I don't think it obtains to any great extent.'

'Well,' said he, with a shrug and a smile, 'I wish some good angel would influence my friend in the right direction. I rashly promised his mother and sister in Norfolk to see it done, and he promised them that he would do it. But I suppose he never will.'

He spoke for a minute or two on indifferent topics, and went away.

I had scarcely unlocked the drawers of my writing-table next morning, when he reappeared. I noticed that he came straight to the door in the glass partition, and did not pause a single moment outside.

'Can you spare me two minutes, my dear Mr Sampson?'

'By all means.'

'Much obliged,' laying his hat and umbrella on the table; 'I came early, not to interrupt you. The fact is, I am taken by surprise in reference to this proposal my friend has made.'

'Has he made one?' said I.

'Ye-es,' he answered, deliberately looking at me; and then a bright idea seemed to strike him—'or he only tells me he has. Perhaps that may be a new way of evading the matter. By Jupiter, I never thought of that!'

Mr Adams was opening the morning's letters in the outer office. 'What is the name, Mr Slinkton?' I asked.

'Beckwith.'

I looked out at the door and requested Mr Adams, if there were a proposal in that name, to bring it in. He had already laid it out of his hand on the counter.

It was easily selected from the rest, and he gave it me. Alfred Beckwith. Proposal to effect a policy with us for two thousand pounds. Dated yesterday.

'From the Middle Temple, I see, Mr Slinkton.'

'Yes. He lives on the same staircase with me; his door is opposite. I never thought he would make me his reference though.'

'It seems natural enough that he should.'

'Quite so, Mr Sampson; but I never thought of it. Let me see.' He took the printed paper from his pocket. 'How am I to answer all these questions?'

'According to the truth, of course,' said I.

'O, of course!' he answered, looking up from the paper with a smile; 'I meant they were so many. But you do right to be particular. It stands to reason that you must be particular. Will you allow me to use your pen and ink?'

'Certainly.'

'And your desk?'

'Certainly.'

He had been hovering about between his hat and his umbrella for a place to write on. He now sat down in my chair, at my blotting- paper and inkstand, with the long walk up his head in accurate perspective before me, as I stood with my back to the fire.

Before answering each question he ran over it aloud, and discussed it. How long had he known Mr Alfred Beckwith? That he had to calculate by years upon his fingers. What were his habits? No difficulty about them; temperate in the last degree, and took a little too much exercise, if anything. All the answers were satisfactory. When he had written them all, he looked them over, and finally signed them in a very pretty hand. He supposed he had now done with the business. I told him he was not likely to be troubled any farther. Should he leave the papers there? If he pleased. Much obliged. Good-morning.

I had had one other visitor before him; not at the office, but at my own house. That visitor had come to my bedside when it was not yet daylight, and had been seen by no one else but by my faithful confidential servant.

A second reference paper (for we required always two) was sent down into Norfolk, and was duly received back by post. This, likewise, was satisfactorily answered in every respect. Our forms were all complied with; we accepted the proposal, and the premium for one year was paid.

For six or seven months I saw no more of Mr Slinkton. He called once at my house, but I was not at home; and he once asked me to dine with him in the Temple, but I was engaged. His friend's assurance was effected in March. Late in September or early in October I was down at Scarborough for a breath of sea-air, where I met him on the beach. It was a hot evening; he came toward me with his hat in his hand; and there was the walk I had felt so strongly disinclined to take in perfect order again, exactly in front of the bridge of my nose.

He was not alone, but had a young lady on his arm.

She was dressed in mourning, and I looked at her with great interest. She had the appearance of being extremely delicate, and her face was remarkably pale and melancholy; but she was very pretty. He introduced her as his niece, Miss Niner.

'Are you strolling, Mr Sampson? Is it possible you can be idle?'

It WAS possible, and I WAS strolling.

'Shall we stroll together?'

'With pleasure.

The young lady walked between us, and we walked on the cool sea sand, in the direction of Filey.

'There have been wheels here,' said Mr Slinkton. 'And now I look again, the wheels of a hand-carriage! Margaret, my love, your shadow without doubt!'

'Miss Niner's shadow?' I repeated, looking down at it on the sand.

'Not that one,' Mr Slinkton returned, laughing. 'Margaret, my dear, tell Mr Sampson.'

'Indeed,' said the young lady, turning to me, 'there is nothing to tell—except that I constantly see the same invalid old gentleman at all times, wherever I go. I have mentioned it to my uncle, and he calls the gentleman my shadow.'

'Does he live in Scarborough?' I asked.

'He is staying here.'

'Do you live in Scarborough?'

'No, I am staying here. My uncle has placed me with a family here, for my health.'

'And your shadow?' said I, smiling.

'My shadow,' she answered, smiling too, 'is—like myself—not very robust, I fear; for I lose my shadow sometimes, as my shadow loses me at other times. We both seem liable to confinement to the house. I have not seen my shadow for days and days; but it does oddly happen, occasionally, that wherever I go, for many days together, this gentleman goes. We have come together in the most unfrequented nooks on this shore.'

'Is this he?' said I, pointing before us.

The wheels had swept down to the water's edge, and described a great loop on the sand in turning. Bringing the loop back towards us, and spinning it out as it came, was a hand-carriage, drawn by a man.

'Yes,' said Miss Niner, 'this really is my shadow, uncle.'

As the carriage approached us and we approached the carriage, I saw within it an old man, whose head was sunk on his breast, and who was enveloped in a variety of wrappers. He was drawn by a very quiet but very keen-looking man, with iron-gray hair, who was slightly lame. They had passed us, when the carriage stopped, and the old gentleman within, putting out his arm, called to me by my name. I went back, and was absent from Mr Slinkton and his niece for about five minutes.

When I rejoined them, Mr Slinkton was the first to speak. Indeed, he said to me in a raised voice before I came up with him:

'It is well you have not been longer, or my niece might have died of curiosity to know who her shadow is, Mr Sampson.'

'An old East India Director,' said I. 'An intimate friend of our friend's, at whose house I first had the pleasure of meeting you. A certain Major Banks. You have heard of him?'

'Never.'

'Very rich, Miss Niner; but very old, and very crippled. An amiable man, sensible—much interested in you. He has just been expatiating on the affection that he has observed to exist between you and your uncle.'

Mr Slinkton was holding his hat again, and he passed his hand up the straight walk, as if he himself went up it serenely, after me.

'Mr Sampson,' he said, tenderly pressing his niece's arm in his, 'our affection was always a strong one, for we have had but few near ties. We have still fewer now. We have associations to bring us together, that are not of this world, Margaret.'

'Dear uncle!' murmured the young lady, and turned her face aside to hide her tears.

'My niece and I have such remembrances and regrets in common, Mr Sampson,' he feelingly pursued, 'that it would be strange indeed if the relations between us were cold or indifferent. If I remember a conversation we once had together, you will understand the reference I make. Cheer up, dear Margaret. Don't droop, don't droop. My Margaret! I cannot bear to see you droop!'

The poor young lady was very much affected, but controlled herself. His feelings, too, were very acute. In a word, he found himself under such great need of a restorative, that he presently went away, to take a bath of sea-water, leaving the young lady and me sitting by a point of rock, and probably presuming—but that you will say was a pardonable indulgence in a luxury—that she would praise him with all her heart.

She did, poor thing! With all her confiding heart, she praised him to me, for his care of her dead sister, and for his untiring devotion in her last illness. The sister had wasted away very slowly, and wild and terrible fantasies had come over her toward the end, but he had never been impatient with her, or at a loss; had always been gentle, watchful, and self-possessed. The sister had known him, as she had known him, to be the best of men, the kindest of men, and yet a man of such admirable strength of character, as to be a very tower for the support of their weak natures while their poor lives endured.

'I shall leave him, Mr Sampson, very soon,' said the young lady; 'I know my life is drawing to an end; and when I am gone, I hope he will marry and be happy. I am sure he has lived single so long, only for my sake, and for my poor, poor sister's.'

The little hand-carriage had made another great loop on the damp sand, and was coming back again, gradually spinning out a slim figure of eight, half a mile long.

'Young lady,' said I, looking around, laying my hand upon

her arm, and speaking in a low voice, 'time presses. You hear the gentle murmur of that sea?'

She looked at me with the utmost wonder and alarm, saying, 'Yes!'

'And you know what a voice is in it when the storm comes?'

'Yes!'

'You see how quiet and peaceful it lies before us, and you know what an awful sight of power without pity it might be, this very night!'

'Yes!'

'But if you had never heard or seen it, or heard of it in its cruelty, could you believe that it beats every inanimate thing in its way to pieces, without mercy, and destroys life without remorse?'

'You terrify me, sir, by these questions!'

'To save you, young lady, to save you! For God's sake, collect your strength and collect your firmness! If you were here alone, and hemmed in by the rising tide on the flow to fifty feet above your head, you could not be in greater danger than the danger you are now to be saved from.'

The figure on the sand was spun out, and straggled off into a crooked little jerk that ended at the cliff very near us.

'As I am, before Heaven and the Judge of all mankind, your friend, and your dead sister's friend, I solemnly entreat you, Miss Niner, without one moment's loss of time, to come to this gentleman with me!'

If the little carriage had been less near to us, I doubt if I could have got her away; but it was so near that we were there before she had recovered the hurry of being urged from the rock. I did not remain there with her two minutes.

Certainly within five, I had the inexpressible satisfaction of seeing her—from the point we had sat on, and to which I had returned—half supported and half carried up some rude steps notched in the cliff, by the figure of an active man. With that figure beside her, I knew she was safe anywhere.

I sat alone on the rock, awaiting Mr Slinkton's return. The twilight was deepening and the shadows were heavy, when he came round the point, with his hat hanging at his button-hole, smoothing his wet hair with one of his hands, and picking out the old path with the other and a pocket-comb.

'My niece not here, Mr Sampson?' he said, looking about.

'Miss Niner seemed to feel a chill in the air after the sun was down, and has gone home.'

He looked surprised, as though she were not accustomed to do anything without him; even to originate so slight a proceeding.

'I persuaded Miss Niner,' I explained.

'Ah!' said he. 'She is easily persuaded—for her good. Thank you, Mr Sampson; she is better within doors. The bathing place was farther than I thought, to say the truth.'

'Miss Niner is very delicate,' I observed.

He shook his head and drew a deep sigh. 'Very, very, very. You may recollect my saying so. The time that has since intervened has not strengthened her. The gloomy shadow that fell upon her sister so early in life seems, in my anxious eyes, to gather over her, ever darker, ever darker. Dear Margaret, dear Margaret! But we must hope.'

The hand-carriage was spinning away before us at a most indecorous pace for an invalid vehicle, and was making most irregular curves upon the sand. Mr Slinkton, noticing it after he had put his handkerchief to his eyes, said;

'If I may judge from appearances, your friend will be upset, Mr Sampson.'

'It looks probable, certainly,' said I.

'The servant must be drunk.'

'The servants of old gentlemen will get drunk sometimes,' said I.

'The major draws very light, Mr Sampson.'

'The major does draw light,' said I.

By this time the carriage, much to my relief, was lost in the darkness. We walked on for a little, side by side over the sand, in silence. After a short while he said, in a voice still affected by the emotion that his niece's state of health had awakened in him,

'Do you stay here long, Mr Sampson?'

'Why, no. I am going away tonight.'

'So soon? But business always holds you in request. Men like Mr Sampson are too important to others, to be spared to their own need of relaxation and enjoyment.'

'I don't know about that,' said I. 'However, I am going back.'

'To London?'

'To London.'

'I shall be there too, soon after you.'

I knew that as well as he did. But I did not tell him so. Any more than I told him what defensive weapon my right hand rested on in my pocket, as I walked by his side. Any more than I told him why I did not walk on the sea side of him with the night closing in.

We left the beach, and our ways diverged. We exchanged goodnight, and had parted indeed, when he said, returning,

'Mr Sampson, may I ask? Poor Meltham, whom we spoke of,—dead yet?'

'Not when I last heard of him; but too broken a man to live long, and hopelessly lost to his old calling.'

'Dear, dear, dear!' said he, with great feeling. 'Sad, sad, sad! The world is a grave!' And so went his way.

It was not his fault if the world were not a grave; but I did not call that observation after him, any more than I had mentioned those other things just now enumerated. He went his way, and I went mine with all expedition. This happened, as I have said, either at the end of September or beginning of October. The next time I saw him, and the last time, was late in November.

I had a very particular engagement to breakfast in the Temple.

It was a bitter north-easterly morning, and the sleet and slush lay inches deep in the streets. I could get no conveyance, and was soon wet to the knees; but I should have been true to that appointment, though I had to wade to it up to my neck in the same impediments.

The appointment took me to some chambers in the Temple. They were at the top of a lonely corner house overlooking the river. The name, MR ALFRED BECKWITH, was painted on the outer door. On the door opposite, on the same landing, the name MR JULIUS SLINKTON. The doors of both sets of chambers stood open, so that anything said aloud in one set could be heard in the other.

I had never been in those chambers before. They were dismal, close, unwholesome, and oppressive; the furniture, originally good, and not yet old, was faded and dirty,—the rooms were in great disorder; there was a strong prevailing smell of opium, brandy, and tobacco; the grate and fire-irons were splashed all over with unsightly blotches of rust; and on a sofa by the fire, in the room where breakfast had been prepared, lay the host, Mr Beckwith, a man with all the appearances of the worst kind of drunkard, very far advanced upon his shameful way to death.

'Slinkton is not come yet,' said this creature, staggering up when I went in; 'I'll call him.—Halloa! Julius Caesar! Come and drink!' As he hoarsely roared this out, he beat the poker and tongs together in a mad way, as if that were his usual manner of summoning his associate.

The voice of Mr Slinkton was heard through the clatter from the opposite side of the staircase, and he came in. He had not expected the pleasure of meeting me. I have seen several artful men brought to a stand, but I never saw a man so aghast as he was when his eyes rested on mine.

'Julius Caesar,' cried Beckwith, staggering between us, 'Mist' Sampson! Mist' Sampson, Julius Caesar! Julius, Mist' Sampson, is the friend of my soul. Julius keeps me plied with liquor, morning, noon, and night. Julius is a real benefactor. Julius threw the tea and coffee out of window when I used to have any. Julius empties all the water-jugs of their contents, and fills 'em with spirits. Julius winds me up and keeps me going.—Boil the brandy, Julius!'

There was a rusty and furred saucepan in the ashes,—the ashes looked like the accumulation of weeks,—and Beckwith, rolling and staggering between us as if he were going to plunge headlong into the fire, got the saucepan out, and tried to force it into Slinkton's hand.

'Boil the brandy, Julius Caesar! Come! Do your usual office. Boil the brandy!'

He became so fierce in his gesticulations with the saucepan, that I expected to see him lay open Slinkton's head with it. I therefore put out my hand to check him. He reeled back to the sofa, and sat there panting, shaking, and red-eyed, in his rags of dressing-gown, looking at us both.

I noticed then that there was nothing to drink on the table but brandy, and nothing to eat but salted herrings, and a hot, sickly, highly-peppered stew.

'At all events, Mr Sampson,' said Slinkton, offering me the smooth gravel path for the last time, 'I thank you for interfering between me and this unfortunate man's violence. However you came here, Mr Sampson, or with whatever motive you came here, at least I thank you for that.'

'Boil the brandy,' muttered Beckwith.

Without gratifying his desire to know how I came there, I said, quietly, 'How is your niece, Mr Slinkton?'

He looked hard at me, and I looked hard at him.

'I am sorry to say, Mr Sampson, that my niece has proved treacherous and ungrateful to her best friend. She left me without a word of notice or explanation. She was misled, no doubt, by some designing rascal. Perhaps you may have heard of it.'

'I did hear that she was misled by a designing rascal. In fact,

I have proof of it.'

'Are you sure of that?' said he.

'Quite.'

'Boil the brandy,' muttered Beckwith. 'Company to breakfast, Julius Caesar. Do your usual office,—provide the usual breakfast, dinner, tea, and supper. Boil the brandy!'

The eyes of Slinkton looked from him to me, and he said, after a moment's consideration,

'Mr Sampson, you are a man of the world, and so am I. I will be plain with you.'

'O no, you won't,' said I, shaking my head.

'I tell you, sir, I will be plain with you.'

'And I tell you you will not,' said I. 'I know all about you. You plain with any one? Nonsense, nonsense!'

'I plainly tell you, Mr Sampson,' he went on, with a manner almost composed, 'that I understand your object. You want to save your funds, and escape from your liabilities; these are old tricks of trade with you Office gentlemen. But you will not do it, sir; you will not succeed. You have not an easy adversary to play against, when you play against me. We shall have to inquire, in due time, when and how Mr Beckwith fell into his present habits. With that remark, sir, I put this poor creature, and his incoherent wanderings of speech, aside, and wish you a good morning and a better case next time.'

While he was saying this, Beckwith had filled a half-pint glass with brandy. At this moment, he threw the brandy at his face, and threw the glass after it. Slinkton put his hands up, half blinded with the spirit, and cut with the glass across the forehead. At the sound of the breakage, a fourth person came into the room, closed the door, and stood at it; he was a very quiet but very keen-looking man, with iron-gray hair, and slightly lame.

Slinkton pulled out his handkerchief, assuaged the pain in his smarting eyes, and dabbled the blood on his forehead. He was a long time about it, and I saw that in the doing of it, a tremendous change came over him, occasioned by the change in Beckwith,—who ceased to pant and tremble, sat upright, and never took his eyes off him. I never in my life saw a face in which abhorrence and determination were so forcibly painted as in Beckwith's then.

'Look at me, you villain,' said Beckwith, 'and see me as I really am. I took these rooms, to make them a trap for you. I came into them as a drunkard, to bait the trap for you. You fell into the trap, and you will never leave it alive. On the morning when you last went to Mr Sampson's office, I had seen him first.

Your plot has been known to both of us, all along, and you have been counter-plotted all along. What? Having been cajoled into putting that prize of two thousand pounds in your power, I was to be done to death with brandy, and, brandy not proving quick enough, with something quicker? Have I never seen you, when you thought my senses gone, pouring from your little bottle into my glass? Why, you Murderer and Forger, alone here with you in the dead of night, as I have so often been, I have had my hand upon the trigger of a pistol, twenty times, to blow your brains out!'

This sudden starting up of the thing that he had supposed to be his imbecile victim into a determined man, with a settled resolution to hunt him down and be the death of him, mercilessly expressed from head to foot, was, in the first shock, too much for him. Without any figure of speech, he staggered under it. But there is no greater mistake than to suppose that a man who is a calculating criminal, is, in any phase of his guilt, otherwise than true to himself, and perfectly consistent with his whole character. Such a man commits murder, and murder is the natural culmination of his course; such a man has to outface murder, and will do it with hardihood and effrontery. It is a sort of fashion to express surprise that any notorious criminal, having such crime upon his conscience, can so brave it out. Do you think that if he had it on his conscience at all, or had a conscience to have it upon, he would ever have committed the crime?

Perfectly consistent with himself, as I believe all such monsters to be, this Slinkton recovered himself, and showed a defiance that was sufficiently cold and quiet. He was white, he was haggard, he was changed; but only as a sharper who had played for a great stake and had been outwitted and had lost the game.

'Listen to me, you villain,' said Beckwith, 'and let every word you hear me say be a stab in your wicked heart. When I took these rooms, to throw myself in your way and lead you on to the scheme that I knew my appearance and supposed character and habits would suggest to such a devil, how did I know that? Because you were no stranger to me. I knew you well. And I knew you to be the cruel wretch who, for so much money, had killed one innocent girl while she trusted him implicitly, and who was by inches killing another.'

Slinkton took out a snuff-box, took a pinch of snuff, and laughed.

'But see here,' said Beckwith, never looking away, never raising his voice, never relaxing his face, never unclenching his hand.

'See what a dull wolf you have been, after all! The infatuated drunkard who never drank a fiftieth part of the liquor you plied him with, but poured it away, here, there, everywhere—almost before your eyes; who bought over the fellow you set to watch him and to ply him, by outbidding you in his bribe, before he had been at his work three days—with whom you have observed no caution, yet who was so bent on ridding the earth of you as a wild beast, that he would have defeated you if you had been ever so prudent—that drunkard whom you have, many a time, left on the floor of this room, and who has even let you go out of it, alive and undeceived, when you have turned him over with your foot—has, almost as often, on the same night, within an hour, within a few minutes, watched you awake, had his hand at your pillow when you were asleep, turned over your papers, taken samples from your bottles and packets of powder, changed their contents, rifled every secret of your life!'

He had had another pinch of snuff in his hand, but had gradually let it drop from between his fingers to the floor; where he now smoothed it out with his foot, looking down at it the while.

'That drunkard,' said Beckwith, 'who had free access to your rooms at all times, that he might drink the strong drinks that you left in his way and be the sooner ended, holding no more terms with you than he would hold with a tiger, has had his master-key for all your locks, his test for all your poisons, his clue to your cipher- writing. He can tell you, as well as you can tell him, how long it took to complete that deed, what doses there were, what intervals, what signs of gradual decay upon mind and body; what distempered fancies were produced, what observable changes, what physical pain. He can tell you, as well as you can tell him, that all this was recorded day by day, as a lesson of experience for future service. He can tell you, better than you can tell him, where that journal is at this moment.'

Slinkton stopped the action of his foot, and looked at Beckwith.

'No,' said the latter, as if answering a question from him. 'Not in the drawer of the writing-desk that opens with a spring; it is not there, and it never will be there again.'

'Then you are a thief!' said Slinkton.

Without any change whatever in the inflexible purpose, which it was quite terrific even to me to contemplate, and from the power of which I had always felt convinced it was impossible for this wretch to escape, Beckwith returned,

'And I am your niece's shadow, too.'

With an imprecation Slinkton put his hand to his head, tore out some hair, and flung it to the ground. It was the end of the smooth walk; he destroyed it in the action, and it will soon be seen that his use for it was past.

Beckwith went on: 'Whenever you left here, I left here. Although I understood that you found it necessary to pause in the completion of that purpose, to avert suspicion, still I watched you close, with the poor confiding girl. When I had the diary, and could read it word by word,—it was only about the night before your last visit to Scarborough,—you remember the night? you slept with a small flat vial tied to your wrist,—I sent to Mr Sampson, who was kept out of view. This is Mr Sampson's trusty servant standing by the door. We three saved your niece among us.'

Slinkton looked at us all, took an uncertain step or two from the place where he had stood, returned to it, and glanced about him in a very curious way,—as one of the meaner reptiles might, looking for a hole to hide in. I noticed at the same time, that a singular change took place in the figure of the man,—as if it collapsed within his clothes, and they consequently became ill-shapen and ill-fitting.

'You shall know,' said Beckwith, 'for I hope the knowledge will be bitter and terrible to you, why you have been pursued by one man, and why, when the whole interest that Mr Sampson represents would have expended any money in hunting you down, you have been tracked to death at a single individual's charge. I hear you have had the name of Meltham on your lips sometimes?'

I saw, in addition to those other changes, a sudden stoppage come upon his breathing.

'When you sent the sweet girl whom you murdered (you know with what artfully made-out surroundings and probabilities you sent her) to Meltham's office, before taking her abroad to originate the transaction that doomed her to the grave, it fell to Meltham's lot to see her and to speak with her. It did not fall to his lot to save her, though I know he would freely give his own life to have done it. He admired her;—I would say he loved her fallen. As I ran down the passage, my sister's door was unlocked, and revolved slowly upon its hinges. I stared at it horror-stricken, not knowing what was about to issue from it. By the light of the corridor-lamp I saw my sister appear at the opening, her face blanched with terror, her hands groping for help, her whole figure swaying to and fro like that of a drunkard. I ran to her and threw my arms round her, but at that moment her knees seemed to give way and she fell to the ground. She writhed as one who is in terrible pain, and her limbs were dreadfully convulsed. At first I thought that she had not recognized me, but as I bent over her she suddenly shrieked out in a voice which I shall never forget, "Oh, my God! Helen! It was the band! The speckled band!" There was something else which she would fain have said, and she stabbed with her finger into the air in the direction of the doctor's room, but a fresh convulsion seized her and choked her words. I rushed out, calling loudly for my stepfather, and I met him hastening from his room in his dressing-gown. When he reached my sister's side she was unconscious, and though he poured brandy down her throat and sent for medical aid from the village, all efforts were in vain, for she slowly sank and died without having recovered her consciousness. Such was the dreadful end of my beloved sister.'

'One moment,' said Holmes, 'are you sure about this whistle and metallic sound? Could you swear to it?'

'That was what the county coroner asked me at the inquiry. It is my strong impression that I heard it, and yet, among the crash of the gale and the creaking of an old house, I may possibly have been deceived.'

'Was your sister dressed?'

'No, she was in her night-dress. In her right hand was found the charred stump of a match, and in her left a match-box.'

'Showing that she had struck a light and looked about her when the alarm took place. That is important. And what conclusions did the coroner come to?'

'He investigated the case with great care, for Dr. Roylott's conduct had long been notorious in the county, but he was unable to find any satisfactory cause of death. My evidence showed that the door had been fastened upon the inner side, and the windows were blocked by old-fashioned shutters with broad iron bars, which were secured every night. The walls were carefully sounded, and were shown to be quite solid all round, and the flooring was also thoroughly examined, with the same result. The chimney is wide, but is barred up by four large staples. It is certain, therefore, that my sister was quite alone when she met her end. Besides, there were no marks of any violence upon her.'

'How about poison?'

'The doctors examined her for it, but without success.'

'What do you think that this unfortunate lady died of, then?'

'It is my belief that she died of pure fear and nervous shock, though what it was that frightened her I cannot imagine.'

'Were there gypsies in the plantation at the time?'

'Yes, there are nearly always some there.'

'Ah, and what did you gather from this allusion to a band—a speckled band?'

'Sometimes I have thought that it was merely the wild talk of delirium, sometimes that it may have referred to some band of people, perhaps to these very gypsies in the plantation. I do not know whether the spotted handkerchiefs which so many of them wear over their heads might have suggested the strange adjective which she used.'

Holmes shook his head like a man who is far from being satisfied.

'These are very deep waters,' said he; 'pray go on with your narrative.'

'Two years have passed since then, and my life has been until lately lonelier than ever. A month ago, however, a dear friend, whom I have known for many years, has done me the honour to ask my hand in marriage. His name is Armitage—Percy Armitage—the second son of Mr Armitage, of Crane Water, near Reading. My stepfather has offered no opposition to the match, and we are to be married in the course of the spring. Two days ago some repairs were started in the west wing of the building, and my bedroom wall has been pierced, so that I have had to move into the chamber in which my sister died, and to sleep in the very bed in which she slept. Imagine, then, my thrill of terror when last night, as I lay awake, thinking over her terrible fate, I suddenly heard in the silence of the night the low whistle which had been the herald of her own death. I sprang up and lit the lamp, but nothing was to be seen in the room. I was too shaken to go to bed again, however, so I dressed, and as soon as it was daylight I slipped down, got a dog-cart at the Crown Inn, which is opposite, and drove to Leatherhead, from whence I have come on this morning with the one object of seeing you and asking your advice.'

'You have done wisely,' said my friend. 'But have you told me all?'

'Yes, all.'

'Miss Roylott, you have not. You are screening your stepfather.'

'Why, what do you mean?'

For answer Holmes pushed back the frill of black lace which fringed the hand that lay upon our visitor's knee. Five little livid spots, the marks of four fingers and a thumb, were printed upon the white wrist.

'You have been cruelly used,' said Holmes.

The lady coloured deeply and covered over her injured wrist. 'He is a hard man,' she said, 'and perhaps he hardly knows his own strength.'

There was a long silence, during which Holmes leaned his chin upon his hands and stared into the crackling fire.

'This is a very deep business,' he said at last. 'There are a thousand details which I should desire to know before I decide upon our course of action. Yet we have not a moment to lose. If we were to come to Stoke Moran today, would it be possible for us to see over these rooms without the knowledge of your stepfather?'

'As it happens, he spoke of coming into town today upon some most important business. It is probable that he will be away all day, and that there would be nothing to disturb you. We have a housekeeper now, but she is old and foolish, and I could easily get her out of the way.'

'Excellent. You are not averse to this trip, Watson?'

'By no means.'

'Then we shall both come. What are you going to do yourself?'

'I have one or two things which I would wish to do now that I am in town. But I shall return by the twelve o'clock train, so as to be there in time for your coming.'

'And you may expect us early in the afternoon. I have myself some small business matters to attend to. Will you not wait and breakfast?'

'No, I must go. My heart is lightened already since I have confided my trouble to you. I shall look forward to seeing you again this afternoon.' She dropped her thick black veil over her face and glided from the room.

'And what do you think of it all, Watson?' asked Sherlock Holmes, leaning back in his chair.

'It seems to me to be a most dark and sinister business.'

'Dark enough and sinister enough.'

'Yet if the lady is correct in saying that the flooring and walls are sound, and that the door, window, and chimney are impassable, then her sister must have been undoubtedly alone when she met her mysterious end.'

'What becomes, then, of these nocturnal whistles, and what of the very peculiar words of the dying woman?'

'I cannot think.'

'When you combine the ideas of whistles at night, the

presence of a band of gypsies who are on intimate terms with this old doctor, the fact that we have every reason to believe that the doctor has an interest in preventing his stepdaughter's marriage, the dying allusion to a band, and, finally, the fact that Miss Helen Stoner heard a metallic clang, which might have been caused by one of those metal bars that secured the shutters falling back into its place, I think that there is good ground to think that the mystery may be cleared along those lines.'

'But what, then, did the gypsies do?'

'I cannot imagine.'

'I see many objections to any such theory.'

'And so do I. It is precisely for that reason that we are going to Stoke Moran this day. I want to see whether the objections are fatal, or if they may be explained away. But what in the name of the devil!'

The ejaculation had been drawn from my companion by the fact that our door had been suddenly dashed open, and that a huge man had framed himself in the aperture. His costume was a peculiar mixture of the professional and of the agricultural, having a black top-hat, a long frock-coat, and a pair of high gaiters, with a hunting-crop swinging in his hand. So tall was he that his hat actually brushed the cross bar of the doorway, and his breadth seemed to span it across from side to side. A large face, seared with a thousand wrinkles, burned yellow with the sun, and marked with every evil passion, was turned from one to the other of us, while his deep-set, bile-shot eyes, and his high, thin, fleshless nose, gave him somewhat the resemblance to a fierce old bird of prey.

'Which of you is Holmes?' asked this apparition.

'My name, sir; but you have the advantage of me,' said my companion quietly.

'I am Dr. Grimesby Roylott, of Stoke Moran.'

'Indeed, Doctor,' said Holmes blandly. 'Pray take a seat.'

'I will do nothing of the kind. My stepdaughter has been here.

I have traced her. What has she been saying to you?'

'It is a little cold for the time of the year,' said Holmes.

'What has she been saying to you?' screamed the old man furiously.

'But I have heard that the crocuses promise well,' continued my companion imperturbably.

'Ha! You put me off, do you?' said our new visitor, taking a step forward and shaking his hunting-crop. 'I know you, you scoundrel! I have heard of you before. You are Holmes, the meddler.'

My friend smiled.

'Holmes, the busybody!'

His smile broadened.

'Holmes, the Scotland Yard Jack-in-office!'

Holmes chuckled heartily. 'Your conversation is most entertaining,' said he. 'When you go out close the door, for there is a decided draught.'

'I will go when I have said my say. Don't you dare to meddle with my affairs. I know that Miss Stoner has been here. I traced her! I am a dangerous man to fall foul of! See here.' He stepped swiftly forward, seized the poker, and bent it into a curve with his huge brown hands.

'See that you keep yourself out of my grip,' he snarled, and hurling the twisted poker into the fireplace he strode out of the room.

'He seems a very amiable person,' said Holmes, laughing. 'I am not quite so bulky, but if he had remained I might have shown him that my grip was not much more feeble than his own.' As he spoke he picked up the steel poker and, with a sudden effort, straightened it out again.

'Fancy his having the insolence to confound me with the official detective force! This incident gives zest to our investigation, however, and I only trust that our little friend will not suffer from her imprudence in allowing this brute to trace her. And now,

Watson, we shall order breakfast, and afterwards I shall walk down to Doctors' Commons, where I hope to get some data which may help us in this matter.'

It was nearly one o'clock when Sherlock Holmes returned from his excursion. He held in his hand a sheet of blue paper, scrawled over with notes and figures.

'I have seen the will of the deceased wife,' said he. 'To determine its exact meaning I have been obliged to work out the present prices of the investments with which it is concerned. The total income, which at the time of the wife's death was little short of £1100, is now, through the fall in agricultural prices, not more than £750. Each daughter can claim an income of £250, in case of marriage. It is evident, therefore, that if both girls had married, this beauty would have had a mere pittance, while even one of them would cripple him to a very serious extent. My morning's work has not been wasted, since it has proved that he has the very strongest motives for standing in the way of anything of the sort. And now, Watson, this is too serious for dawdling, especially as the old man is aware that we are interesting ourselves in his affairs; so if you are ready, we shall call a cab and drive to Waterloo. I should be very much obliged if you would slip your revolver into your pocket. An Eley's No. 2 is an excellent argument with gentlemen who can twist steel pokers into knots. That and a tooth-brush are, I think all that we need.'

At Waterloo we were fortunate in catching a train for Leatherhead, where we hired a trap at the station inn and drove for four or five miles through the lovely Surrey laries. It was a perfect day, with a bright sun and a few fleecy clouds in the heavens. The trees and wayside hedges were just throwing out their first green shoots, and the air was full of the pleasant smell of the moist earth. To me at least there was a strange contrast between the sweet promise of the spring and this sinister quest upon which we were engaged. My companion sat in the front of the trap, his arms folded, his hat pulled down over his eyes, and his chin sunk upon his breast, buried in the deepest thought. Suddenly, however, he started, tapped me on the shoulder, and pointed over the meadows.

'Look there!' said he.

A heavily timbered park stretched up in a gentle slope, thickening into a grove at the highest point. From amid the branches there jutted out the gray gables and high roof-tree of a very old mansion.

'Stoke Moran?' said he.

'Yes, sir, that be the house of Dr. Grimesby Roylott,' remarked the driver.

'There is some building going on there,' said Holmes; 'that is where we are going.'

'There's the village,' said the driver, pointing to a cluster of roofs some distance to the left; 'but if you want to get to the house, you'll find it shorter to get over this stile, and so by the footpath over the fields. There it is, where the lady is walking.'

'And the lady, I fancy, is Miss Stoner,' observed Holmes, shading his eyes. 'Yes, I think we had better do as you suggest.'

We got off, paid our fare, and the trap rattled back on its way to Leatherhead.

'I thought it as well,' said Holmes as we climbed the stile, 'that this fellow should think we had come here as architects, or on some definite business. It may stop his gossip. Good-afternoon, Miss Stoner. You see that we have been as good as our word.'

Our client of the morning had hurried forward to meet us with a face which spoke her joy. 'I have been waiting so eagerly for you,' she cried, shaking hands with us warmly. 'All has turned out splendidly. Dr. Roylott has gone to town, and it is unlikely that he will be back before evening.'

'We have had the pleasure of making the doctor's acquaintance,' said Holmes, and in a few words he sketched out what had occurred. Miss Stoner turned white to the lips as she listened.

'Good heavens!' she cried, 'he has followed me, then.'

'So it appears.'

'He is so cunning that I never know when I am safe from him. What will he say when he returns?'

'He must guard himself, for he may find that there is someone more cunning than himself upon his track. You must lock yourself up from him tonight. If he is violent, we shall take you away to your aunt's at Harrow. Now, we must make the best use of our time, so kindly take us at once to the rooms which we are to examine.'

The building was of gray, lichen-blotched stone, with a high central portion and two curving wings, like the claws of a crab, thrown out on each side. In one of these wings the windows were broken and blocked with wooden boards, while the roof was partly caved in, a picture of ruin. The central portion was in little better repair, but the right-hand block was comparatively modern, and the blinds in the windows, with the blue smoke curling up from the chimneys, showed that this was where the family resided. Some scaffolding had been erected against the end wall, and the stone-work had been broken into, but there were no signs of any workmen at the moment of our visit. Holmes walked slowly up and down the ill-trimmed lawn and examined with deep attention the outsides of the windows.

'This, I take it, belongs to the room in which you used to sleep, the centre one to your sister's, and the one next to the main building to Dr. Roylott's chamber?'

'Exactly so. But I am now sleeping in the middle one.'

'Pending the alterations, as I understand. By the way, there does not seem to be any very pressing need for repairs at that end wall.'

'There were none. I believe that it was an excuse to move me from my room.'

'Ah! That is suggestive. Now, on the other side of this narrow wing runs the corridor from which these three rooms open. There are windows in it, of course?' 'Yes, but very small ones. Too narrow for anyone to pass through.'

'As you both locked your doors at night, your rooms were unapproachable from that side. Now, would you have the kindness to go into your room and bar your shutters?'

Miss Stoner did so, and Holmes, after a careful examination through the open window, endeavoured in every way to force the shutter open, but without success. There was no slit through which a knife could be passed to raise the bar. Then with his lens he tested the hinges, but they were of solid iron, built firmly into the massive masonry. 'Hum!' said he, scratching his chin in some perplexity, 'my theory certainly presents some difficulties. No one could pass these shutters if they were bolted. Well, we shall see if the inside throws any light upon the matter.'

A small side door led into the whitewashed corridor from which the three bedrooms opened. Holmes refused to examine the third chamber, so we passed at once to the second, that in which Miss Stoner was now sleeping, and in which her sister had met with her fate. It was a homely little room, with a low ceiling and a gaping fireplace, after the fashion of old country-houses. A brown chest of drawers stood in one corner, a narrow white-counterpaned bed in another, and a dressing-table on the left-hand side of the window. These articles, with two small wicker-work chairs, made up all the furniture in the room save for a square of Wilton carpet in the centre. The boards round and the panelling of the walls were of brown, worm-eaten oak, so old and discoloured that it may have dated from the original building of the house. Holmes drew one of the chairs into a corner and sat silent, while his eyes travelled round and round and up and down, taking in every detail of the apartment.

'Where does that bell communicate with?' he asked, at last, pointing to a thick belt-rope which hung down beside the bed, the tassel actually lying upon the pillow.

'It goes to the housekeeper's room.'

'It looks newer than the other things?'

'Yes, it was only put there a couple of years ago.'

'Your sister asked for it, I suppose?'

'No, I never heard of her using it. We used always to get what we wanted for ourselves.'

'Indeed, it seemed unnecessary to put so nice a bell-pull there. You will excuse me for a few minutes while I satisfy myself as to this floor.' He threw himself down upon his face with his lens in his hand and crawled swiftly backward and forward, examining minutely the cracks between the boards. Then he did the same with the wood-work with which the chamber was panelled. Finally he walked over to the bed and spent some time in staring at it and in running his eye up and down the wall. Finally he took the bell-rope in his hand and gave it a brisk tug.

'Why, it's a dummy,' said he.

'Won't it ring?'

'No, it is not even attached to a wire. This is very interesting. You can see now that it is fastened to a hook just above where the little opening for the ventilator is.'

'How very absurd! I never noticed that before.'

'Very strange!' muttered Holmes, pulling at the rope. 'There are one or two very singular points about this room. For example, what a fool a builder must be to open a ventilator into another room, when, with the same trouble, he might have communicated with the outside air!'

'That is also quite modern,' said the lady.

'Done about the same time as the bell-rope?' remarked Holmes.

'Yes, there were several little changes carried out about that time.'

'They seem to have been of a most interesting character—

dummy bell-ropes, and ventilators which do not ventilate. With your permission, Miss Stoner, we shall now carry our researches into the inner apartment.'

Dr. Grimesby Roylott's chamber was larger than that of his stepdaughter, but was as plainly furnished. A camp-bed, a small wooden shelf full of books, mostly of a technical character, an armchair beside the bed, a plain wooden chair against the wall, a round table, and a large iron safe, were the principal things which met the eye. Holmes walked slowly round and examined each and all of them with the keenest interest.

'What's in here?' he asked, tapping the safe.

'My stepfather's business papers.'

'Oh! You have seen inside, then?'

'Only once, some years ago. I remember that it was full of papers.'

'There isn't a cat in it, for example?'

'No. What a strange idea!'

'Well, look at this!' He took up a small saucer of milk which stood on the top of it.

'No, we don't keep a cat. But there is a cheetah and a baboon.'

'Ah, yes, of course! Well, a cheetah is just a big cat, and yet a saucer of milk does not go very far in satisfying its wants, I daresay. There is one point which I should wish to determine.' He squatted down in front of the wooden chair and examined the seat of it with the greatest attention.

'Thank you. That is quite settled,' said he, rising and putting his lens in his pocket. 'Hello! Here is something interesting!'

The object which had caught his eye was a small dog lash hung on one corner of the bed. The lash, however, was curled upon itself and tied so as to make a loop of whipcord.

'What do you make of that, Watson?'

'It's a common enough lash. But I don't know why if should be tied.'

'That is not quite so common, is it? Ah, me! It's a wicked world, and when a clever man turns his brains to crime it is the worst of all. I think that I have seen enough now, Miss Stoner, and with your permission we shall walk out upon the lawn.'

I had never seen my friend's face so grim or his brow so dark as it was when we turned from the scene of this investigation. We had walked several times up and down the lawn, neither Miss Stoner nor myself liking to break in upon his thoughts before he roused himself from his reverie.

'It is very essential, Miss Stoner,' said he, 'that you should absolutely follow my advice in every respect.'

'I shall most certainly do so.'

'The matter is too serious for any hesitation. Your life may depend upon your compliance.'

'I assure you that I am in your hands.'

'In the first place, both my friend and I must spend the night in your room.'

Both Miss Stoner and I gazed at him in astonishment.

'Yes, it must be so. Let me explain. I believe that that is the village inn over there?'

'Yes, that is the Crown.'

'Very good. Your windows would be visible from there?'

'Certainly.'

'You must confine yourself to your room, on pretence of a headache, when your stepfather comes back. Then when you hear him retire for the night, you must open the shutters of your window, undo the hasp, put your lamp there as a signal to us, and then withdraw quietly with everything which you are likely to want into the room which you used to occupy. I have no doubt that, in spite of the repairs, you could manage there for one night.'

'Oh, yes, easily.'

'The rest you will leave in our hands.'

'But what will you do?'

'We shall spend the night in your room, and we shall investigate the cause of this noise which has disturbed you.'

'I believe, Mr Holmes, that you have already made up your mind,' said Miss Stoner, laying her hand upon my companion's sleeve.

'Perhaps I have.'

'Then, for pity's sake, tell me what was the cause of my sister's death.'

'I should prefer to have clearer proofs before I speak.'

'You can at least tell me whether my own thought is correct, and if she died from some sudden fright.'

'No, I do not think so. I think that there was probably some more tangible cause. And now, Miss Stoner, we must leave you for if Dr. Roylott returned and saw us our journey would be in vain. Good-bye, and be brave, for if you will do what I have told you you may rest assured that we shall soon drive away the dangers that threaten you.'

Sherlock Holmes and I had no difficulty in engaging a bedroom and sitting-room at the Crown Inn. They were on the upper floor, and from our window we could command a view of the avenue gate, and of the inhabited wing of Stoke Moran Manor House. At dusk we saw Dr. Grimesby Roylott drive past, his huge form looming up beside the little figure of the lad who drove him. The boy had some slight difficulty in undoing the heavy iron gates, and we heard the hoarse roar of the doctor's voice and saw the fury with which he shook his clinched fists at him. The trap drove on, and a few minutes later we saw a sudden light spring up among the trees as the lamp was lit in one of the sitting-rooms.

'Do you know, Watson,' said Holmes as we sat together in the gathering darkness, 'I have really some scruples as to taking you tonight. There is a distinct element of danger.'

'Can I be of assistance?'

'Your presence might be invaluable.'

'Then I shall certainly come.'

'It is very kind of you.'

'You speak of danger. You have evidently seen more in these rooms than was visible to me.'

'No, but I fancy that I may have deduced a little more. I imagine that you saw all that I did.'

'I saw nothing remarkable save the bell-rope, and what purpose that could answer I confess is more than I can imagine.'

'You saw the ventilator, too?'

'Yes, but I do not think that it is such a very unusual thing to have a small opening between two rooms. It was so small that a rat could hardly pass through.'

'I knew that we should find a ventilator before ever we came to Stoke Moran.'

'My dear Holmes!'

'Oh, yes, I did. You remember in her statement she said that her sister could smell Dr. Roylott's cigar. Now, of course that suggested at once that there must be a communication between the two rooms. It could only be a small one, or it would have been remarked upon at the coroner's inquiry. I deduced a ventilator.'

'But what harm can there be in that?'

'Well, there is at least a curious coincidence of dates. A ventilator is made, a cord is hung, and a lady who sleeps in the bed dies. Does not that strike you?'

'I cannot as yet see any connection.'

'Did you observe anything very peculiar about that bed?'

'No.'

'It was clamped to the floor. Did you ever see a bed fastened like that before?'

'I cannot say that I have.'

'The lady could not move her bed. It must always be in the same relative position to the ventilator and to the rope—or so we may call it, since it was clearly never meant for a bell-pull.'

'Holmes,' I cried, 'I seem to see dimly what you are hinting at. We are only just in time to prevent some subtle and horrible crime.'

'Subtle enough and horrible enough. When a doctor does go wrong he is the first of criminals. He has nerve and he has knowledge. Palmer and Pritchard were among the heads of their profession. This man strikes even deeper, but I think, Watson, that we shall be able to strike deeper still. But we shall have horrors enough before the night is over; for goodness' sake let us have a quiet pipe and turn our minds for a few hours to something more cheerful.'

About nine o'clock the light among the trees was extinguished, and all was dark in the direction of the Manor House. Two hours passed slowly away, and then, suddenly, just at the stroke of eleven, a single bright light shone out right in front of us.

'That is our signal,' said Holmes, springing to his feet; 'it comes from the middle window.'

As we passed out he exchanged a few words with the landlord, explaining that we were going on a late visit to an acquaintance, and that it was possible that we might spend the night there. A moment later we were out on the dark road, a chill wind blowing in our faces, and one yellow light twinkling in front of us through the gloom to guide us on our sombre errand.

There was little difficulty in entering the grounds, for unrepaired breaches gaped in the old park wall. Making our way among the trees, we reached the lawn, crossed it, and were about to enter through the window when out from a clump of laurel bushes there darted what seemed to be a hideous and distorted child, who threw itself upon the grass with writhing limbs and then ran swiftly across the lawn into the darkness.

'My God!' I whispered; 'did you see it?'

Holmes was for the moment as startled as I. His hand closed like a vise upon my wrist in his agitation. Then he broke into a low laugh and put his lips to my ear.

'It is a nice household,' he murmured. 'That is the baboon.'

I had forgotten the strange pets which the doctor affected. There was a cheetah, too; perhaps we might find it upon our shoulders at any moment. I confess that I felt easier in my mind when, after following Holmes's example and slipping off my shoes, I found myself inside the bedroom. My companion noiselessly closed the shutters, moved the lamp onto the table, and cast his eyes round the room. All was as we had seen it in the daytime. Then creeping up to me and making a trumpet of his hand, he whispered into my ear again so gently that it was all that I could do to distinguish the words:

'The least sound would be fatal to our plans.'

I nodded to show that I had heard.

'We must sit without light. He would see it through the ventilator.'

I nodded again.

'Do not go asleep; your very life may depend upon it. Have your pistol ready in case we should need it. I will sit on the side of the bed, and you in that chair.'

I took out my revolver and laid it on the corner of the table.

Holmes had brought up a long thin cane, and this he placed upon the bed beside him. By it he laid the box of matches and the stump of a candle. Then he turned down the lamp, and we were left in darkness.

How shall I ever forget that dreadful vigil? I could not hear a sound, not even the drawing of a breath, and yet I knew that my companion sat open-eyed, within a few feet of me, in the same state of nervous tension in which I was myself. The shutters cut off the least ray of light, and we waited in absolute darkness. From outside came the occasional cry of a night-bird, and once at our very window a long drawn catlike whine, which told us that the cheetah was indeed at liberty. Far away we could hear the deep tones of the parish clock, which boomed out every quarter of an hour. How long they seemed, those quarters! Twelve struck, and one and two and three, and still we sat waiting silently for whatever might befall.

Suddenly there was the momentary gleam of a light up in the direction of the ventilator, which vanished immediately, but was succeeded by a strong smell of burning oil and heated metal. Someone in the next room had lit a dark-lantern. I heard a gentle sound of movement, and then all was silent once more, though the smell grew stronger. For half an hour I sat with straining ears. Then suddenly another sound became audible—a very gentle, soothing sound, like that of a small jet of steam escaping continually from a kettle. The instant that we heard it, Holmes sprang from the bed, struck a match, and lashed furiously with his cane at the bell-pull.

'You see it, Watson?' he yelled. 'You see it?'

But I saw nothing. At the moment when Holmes struck the light I heard a low, clear whistle, but the sudden glare flashing into my weary eyes made it impossible for me to tell what it was at which my friend lashed so savagely. I could, however, see that his face was deadly pale and filled with horror and loathing. He had ceased to strike and was gazing up at the ventilator when suddenly there broke from the silence of the night the most horrible cry to which I have ever listened. It swelled up louder and louder, a hoarse yell of pain and fear and anger all mingled in the one dreadful shriek. They say that away down in the village, and even in the distant parsonage, that cry raised the sleepers from their beds. It struck cold to our hearts, and I stood gazing at Holmes, and he at me, until the last echoes of it had died away into the silence from which it rose.

'What can it mean?' I gasped.

'It means that it is all over,' Holmes answered. 'And perhaps, after all, it is for the best. Take your pistol, and we will enter Dr.

Roylott's room.'

With a grave face he lit the lamp and led the way down the corridor. Twice he struck at the chamber door without any reply from within. Then he turned the handle and entered, I at his heels, with the cocked pistol in my hand.

It was a singular sight which met our eyes. On the table stood a dark-lantern with the shutter half open, throwing a brilliant beam of light upon the iron safe, the door of which was ajar. Beside this table, on the wooden chair, sat Dr. Grimesby Roylott clad in a long gray dressing-gown, his bare ankles protruding beneath, and his feet thrust into red heelless Turkish slippers. Across his lap lay the short stock with the long lash which we had noticed during the day. His chin was cocked upward and his eyes were fixed in a dreadful, rigid stare at the corner of the ceiling. Round his brow he had a peculiar yellow band, with brownish speckles, which seemed to be bound tightly round his head. As we entered he made neither sound nor motion.

'The band! the speckled band!' whispered Holmes.

I took a step forward. In an instant his strange headgear began to move, and there reared itself from among his hair the squat diamond-shaped head and puffed neck of a loathsome serpent.

'It is a swamp adder!' cried Holmes; 'the deadliest snake in India. He has died within ten seconds of being bitten. Violence does, in truth, recoil upon the violent, and the schemer falls into the pit which he digs for another. Let us thrust this creature back into its den, and we can then remove Miss Stoner to some place of shelter and let the county police know what has happened.'

As he spoke he drew the dog-whip swiftly from the dead man's lap, and throwing the noose round the reptile's neck he drew it from its horrid perch and, carrying it at arm's length, threw it into the iron safe, which he closed upon it.

Such are the true facts of the death of Dr. Grimesby Roylott, of Stoke Moran. It is not necessary that I should prolong a narrative which has already run to too great a length by telling how we broke the sad news to the terrified girl, how we conveyed her by the morning train to the care of her good aunt at Harrow, of how the slow process of official inquiry came to the conclusion that the doctor met his fate while indiscreetly playing with a dangerous pet. The little which I had yet to learn of the case was told me by Sherlock Holmes as we travelled back next day.

'I had,' said he, 'come to an entirely erroneous conclusion which shows, my dear Watson, how dangerous it always is to reason from insufficient data. The presence of the gypsies, and the use of the word 'band,' which was used by the poor girl, no doubt to explain the appearance which she had caught a hurried glimpse of by the light of her match, were sufficient to put me upon an entirely wrong scent. I can only claim the merit that I instantly reconsidered my position when, however, it became clear to me that whatever danger threatened an occupant of the room could not come either from the window or the door. My attention was speedily drawn, as I have already remarked to you, to this ventilator, and to the bell-rope which hung down to the bed. The discovery that this was a dummy, and that the bed was clamped to the floor, instantly gave rise to the suspicion that the rope was there as a bridge for something passing through the hole and coming to the bed. The idea of a snake instantly occurred to me, and when I coupled it with my knowledge that the doctor was furnished with a supply of creatures from India, I felt that I was probably on the right track. The idea of using a form of poison which could not possibly be discovered by any chemical test was just such a one as would occur to a clever and ruthless man who had had an Eastern training. The rapidity with which such a poison would take effect would also, from his point of view, be an advantage. It would be a sharp-eyed coroner, indeed, who could distinguish the two little dark punctures which would show where the poison fangs had done their work. Then I thought of the whistle. Of course he must recall the snake before the morning light revealed it to the victim. He had trained it, probably by the use of the milk which we saw, to return to him when summoned. He would put it through this ventilator at the hour that he thought best, with the certainty that it would crawl down the rope and land on the bed. It might or might not bite the occupant, perhaps she might escape every night for a week, but sooner or later she must fall a victim.

'I had come to these conclusions before ever I had entered his room. An inspection of his chair showed me that he had been in the habit of standing on it, which of course would be necessary in order that he should reach the ventilator. The sight of the safe, the saucer of milk, and the loop of whipcord were enough to finally dispel any doubts which may have remained. The metallic clang heard by Miss Stoner was obviously caused by her stepfather hastily closing the door of his safe upon its terrible occupant. Having once made up my mind, you know the steps which I took in order to put the matter to the proof. I heard the creature hiss as I have no doubt that you did also, and I instantly lit the light and attacked it.'

'With the result of driving it through the ventilator.'

'And also with the result of causing it to turn upon its master at the other side. Some of the blows of my cane came home and roused its snakish temper, so that it flew upon the first person it saw. In this way I am no doubt indirectly responsible for Dr. Grimesby Roylott's death, and I cannot say that it is likely to weigh very heavily upon my conscience.'

4

THE ADVENTURE OF THE YELLOW FACE

Sherlock Holmes was a man who seldom took exercise for exercise's sake. Few men were capable of greater muscular effort, and he was undoubtedly one of the finest boxers of his weight that I have ever seen; but he looked upon aimless bodily exertion as a waste of energy, and he seldom bestirred himself save where there was some professional object to be served. Then he was absolutely untiring and indefatigable. That he should have kept himself in training under such circumstances is remarkable, but his diet was usually of the sparest, and his habits were simple to the verge of austerity. Save for the occasional use of cocaine, he had no vices, and he only turned to the drug as a protest against the monotony of existence when cases were scanty and the papers uninteresting.

One day in early spring he had so far relaxed as to go for a walk with me in the Park, where the first faint shoots of green were breaking out upon the elms, and the sticky spear-heads of the chestnuts were just beginning to burst into their five-fold leaves. For two hours we rambled about together, in silence for the most part, as befits two men who know each other intimately. It was nearly five before we were back in Baker Street once more.

'Beg pardon, sir,' said our page-boy as he opened the door. 'There's been a gentleman here asking for you, sir.'

Holmes glanced reproachfully at me. 'So much for afternoon walks!' said he. 'Has this gentleman gone, then?'

'Yes, sir.'

'Didn't you ask him in?'

'Yes, sir, he came in.'

'How long did he wait?'

'Half an hour, sir. He was a very restless gentleman, sir a-walkin' and a-stampin' all the time he was here. I was waitin' outside the door, sir, and I could hear him. At last he outs into the passage, and he cries, "Is that man never goin' to come?" Those were his very words, sir. "You'll only need to wait a little longer," says I. "Then I'll wait in the open air, for I feel half choked," says he. "I'll be back before long." And with that he ups and he outs, and all I could say wouldn't hold him back.'

'Well, well, you did your best,' said Holmes as we walked into our room. 'It's very annoying, though, Watson. I was badly in need of a case, and this looks, from the man's impatience, as if it were of importance. Hullo! That's not your pipe on the table. He must have left his behind him. A nice old brier with a good long stem of what the tobacconists call amber. I wonder how many real amber mouthpieces there are in London? Some people think that a fly in it is a sign. Well, he must have been disturbed in his mind to leave a pipe behind him which he evidently values highly.'

'How do you know that he values it highly?' I asked.

'Well, I should put the original cost of the pipe at seven and sixpence. Now it has, you see, been twice mended, once in the wooden stem and once in the amber. Each of these mends, done, as you observe, with silver bands, must have cost more than the pipe did originally. The man must value the pipe highly when he prefers to patch it up rather than buy a new one with the same money.'

'Anything else?' I asked, for Holmes was turning the pipe about in his hand and staring at it in his peculiar pensive way.

He held it up and tapped on it with his long, thin forefinger, as a professor might who was lecturing on a bone.

'Pipes are occasionally of extraordinary interest,' said he. 'Nothing has more individuality, save perhaps watches and bootlaces. The indications here, however, are neither very marked nor very important. The owner is obviously a muscular man, left-handed, with an excellent set of teeth, careless in his habits, and with no need to practise economy.'

My friend threw out the information in a very offhand way, but I saw that he cocked his eye at me to see if I had followed his reasoning.

'You think a man must be well-to-do if he smokes a seven-shilling pipe?' said I.

'This is Grosvenor mixture at eightpence an ounce,' Holmes answered, knocking a little out on his palm. 'As he might get an excellent smoke for half the price, he has no need to practise economy.'

'And the other points?'

'He has been in the habit of lighting his pipe at lamps and gasjets. You can see that it is quite charred all down one side. Of course a match could not have done that. Why should a man hold a match to the side of his pipe? But you cannot light it at a lamp without getting the bowl charred. And it is all on the right side of the pipe. From that I gather that he is a left-handed man. You hold your own pipe to the lamp and see how naturally you, being right-handed, hold the left side to the flame. You might do it once the other way, but not as a constancy. This has always been held so. Then he has bitten through his amber. It takes a muscular, energetic fellow, and one with a good set of teeth, to do that. But if I am not mistaken I hear him upon the stair, so we shall have something more interesting than his pipe to study.'

An instant later our door opened, and a tall young man entered the room. He was well but quietly dressed in a dark gray suit and carried a brown wideawake in his hand. I should have put him at about thirty, though he was really some years older.

'I beg your pardon,' said he with some embarrassment, 'I suppose I should have knocked. Yes, of course I should have knocked. The fact is that I am a little upset, and you must put it all down to that.' He passed his hand over his forehead like a man who is half dazed, and then fell rather than sat down upon a chair.

'I can see that you have not slept for a night or two,' said Holmes in his easy, genial way. 'That tries a man's nerves more than work, and more even than pleasure. May I ask how I can help you?'

'I wanted your advice, sir. I don't know what to do, and my whole life seems to have gone to pieces.'

'You wish to employ me as a consulting detective?'

'Not that only. I want your opinion as a judicious man—as a man of the world. I want to know what I ought to do next. I hope to God you'll be able to tell me.'

He spoke in little, sharp, jerky outbursts, and it seemed to me that to speak at all was very painful to him, and that his will all through was overriding his inclinations.

'It's a very delicate thing,' said he. 'One does not like to speak of one's domestic affairs to strangers. It seems dreadful to discuss the conduct of one's wife with two men whom I have never seen before. It's horrible to have to do it. But I've got to the end of my tether, and I must have advice.'

'My dear Mr Grant Munro—' began Holmes.

Our visitor sprang from his chair. 'What!' he cried, 'you know my name?'

'If you wish to preserve your incognito,' said Holmes, smiling, 'I would suggest that you cease to write your name upon the lining of your hat, or else that you turn the crown towards the person whom you are addressing. I was about to say that my friend and I have listened to a good many strange secrets in this room, and that we have had the good fortune to bring peace to many troubled souls. I trust that we may do as much for you. Might I beg you, as time may prove to be of importance, to furnish me with the facts of your case without further delay?'

Our visitor again passed his hand over his forehead, as if he found it bitterly hard. From every gesture and expression I could see that he was a reserved, self-contained man, with a dash of pride in his nature, more likely to hide his wounds than to expose them. Then suddenly, with a fierce gesture of his closed hand, like one who throws reserve to the winds, he began:

'The facts are these, Mr Holmes,' said he. 'I am a married man and have been so for three years. During that time my wife and I have loved each other as fondly and lived as happily as any two that ever were joined. We have not had a difference, not one, in thought or word or deed. And now, since last Monday, there has suddenly sprung up a barrier between us, and I find that there is something in her life and in her thoughts of which I know as little as if she were the woman who brushes by me in the street. We are estranged, and I want to know why.

'Now there is one thing that I want to impress upon you before I go any further, Mr Holmes. Effie loves me. Don't let there be any mistake about that. She loves me with her whole heart and soul, and never more than now. I know it. I feel it. I don't want to argue about that. A man can tell easily enough when a woman loves him. But there's this secret between us, and we can never be the same until it is cleared.'

'Kindly let me have the facts, Mr Munro,' said Holmes with some impatience.

'I'll tell you what I know about Effie's history. She was a widow when I met her first, though quite young—only twenty-five. Her name then was Mrs Hebron. She went out to America when she was young and lived in the town of Atlanta, where she married this Hebron, who was a lawyer with a good practice. They had one child, but the yellow fever broke out badly in the place, and both husband and child died of it. I have seen his death certificate. This sickened her of America, and she came back to live with a maiden aunt at Pinner, in Middlesex. I may mention that her husband had left her comfortably off, and that she had a capital of about four thousand five hundred pounds, which had been so well invested by him that it returned an average of seven per cent. She had only been six months at Pinner when I met her; we fell in love with each other, and we married a few weeks afterwards.

'I am a hop merchant myself, and as I have an income of seven or eight hundred, we found ourselves comfortably off and took a nice eighty-pound-a-year villa at Norbury. Our little place was very countrified, considering that it is so close to town. We had an inn and two houses a little above us, and a single cottage at the other side of the field which faces us, and except those there were no houses until you got halfway to the station. My business took me into town at certain seasons, but in summer I had less to do, and then in our country home my wife and I were just as happy as could be wished. I tell you that there never was a shadow between us until this accursed affair began.

'There's one thing I ought to tell you before I go further. When we married, my wife made over all her property to me—rather against my will, for I saw how awkward it would be if my business affairs went wrong. However, she would have it so, and it was done. Well, about six weeks ago she came to me.

'"Jack," said she, "when you took my money you said that if ever I wanted any I was to ask you for it."

'"Certainly" said I. "It's all your own."

'"Well," said she, "I want a hundred pounds."

'I was a bit staggered at this, for I had imagined it was simply a new dress or something of the kind that she was after.

'"What on earth for?" I asked.

'"Oh," said she in her playful way, "you said that you were only my banker, and bankers never ask questions, you know."

'"If you really mean it, of course you shall have the money," said I.

'"Oh, yes, I really mean it."

'"And you won't tell me what you want it for?"

'"Some day, perhaps, but not just at present, Jack."

'So I had to be content with that, though it was the first time that there had ever been any secret between us. I gave her a check, and I never thought any more of the matter. It may have nothing to do with what came afterwards, but I thought it only right to mention it.

'Well, I told you just now that there is a cottage not far from our house. There is just a field between us, but to reach it you have to go along the road and then turn down a lane. Just beyond it is a nice little grove of Scotch firs, and I used to be very fond of strolling down there, for trees are always a neighbourly kind of thing. The cottage had been standing empty this eight months, and it was a pity, for it was a pretty two-storied place, with an old-fashioned porch and a honeysuckle about it. I have stood many a time and thought what a neat little homestead it would make.

'Well, last Monday evening I was taking a stroll down that way when I met an empty van coming up the lane and saw a pile of carpets and things lying about on the grass-plot beside the porch. It was clear that the cottage had at last been let. I walked past it, and then stopping, as an idle man might, I ran my eye over it and wondered what sort of folk they were who had come to live so near us. And as I looked I suddenly became aware that a face was watching me out of one of the upper windows.

'I don't know what there was about that face, Mr Holmes, but it seemed to send a chill right down my back. I was some little way off, so that I could not make out the features, but there was something unnatural and inhuman about the face. That was the impression that I had, and I moved quickly forward to get a nearer view of the person who was watching me. But as I did so the face suddenly disappeared, so suddenly that it seemed to have been plucked away into the darkness of the room. I stood for five minutes thinking the business over and trying to analyze my impressions. I could not tell if the face was that of a man or a woman. It had been too far from me for that. But its colour was what had impressed me most. It was of a livid chalky white, and with something set and rigid about it which was shockingly unnatural. So disturbed was I that I determined to see a little more of the new inmates of the cottage. I approached and knocked at the door, which was instantly opened by a tall, gaunt woman with a harsh, forbidding face.

'"What may you be wantin'?" she asked in a Northern accent.

"I am your neighbour over yonder," said I, nodding towards my house. "I see that you have only just moved in, so I thought that if I could be of any help to you in any—"

'"Ay, we'll just ask ye when we want ye," said she, and shut the door in my face. Annoyed at the churlish rebuff, I turned my back and walked home. All evening, though I tried to think of other things, my mind would still turn to the apparition at the window and the rudeness of the woman. I determined to say nothing about the former to my wife, for she is a nervous, highly strung woman, and I had no wish that she should share the unpleasant impression which had been produced upon myself. I remarked to her, however, before I fell asleep, that the cottage was now occupied, to which she returned no reply.

'I am usually an extremely sound sleeper. It has been a standing jest in the family that nothing could ever wake me during the night. And yet somehow on that particular night, whether it may have been the slight excitement produced by my little adventure or not I know not, but I slept much more lightly than usual. Half in my dreams I was dimly conscious that something was going on in the room, and gradually became aware that my wife had dressed herself and was slipping on her mantle and her bonnet. My lips were parted to murmur out some sleepy words of surprise or remonstrance at this untimely preparation, when suddenly my half-opened eyes fell upon her face, illuminated by the candle-light, and astonishment held me dumb. She wore an expression such as I had never seen before—such as I should have thought her incapable of assuming. She was deadly pale and breathing fast, glancing furtively towards the bed as she fastened her mantle to see if she had disturbed me. Then thinking that I was still asleep, she slipped noiselessly from the room, and an instant later I heard a sharp creaking which could only come from the hinges of the front door. I sat up in bed and rapped my knuckles against the rail to make certain that I was truly awake. Then I took my watch from under the pillow. It was three in the morning. What on this earth could my wife be doing out on the country road at three in the morning?

'I had sat for about twenty minutes turning the thing over in my mind and trying to find some possible explanation. The more I thought, the more extraordinary and inexplicable did it appear. I was still puzzling over it when I heard the door gently close again, and her footsteps coming up the stairs.

'"Where in the world have you been, Effie?" I asked as she entered.

'She gave a violent start and a kind of gasping cry when I spoke, and that cry and start troubled me more than all the rest, for there was something indescribably guilty about them. My wife had always been a woman of a frank, open nature, and it gave me a chill to see her slinking into her own room and crying out and wincing when her own husband spoke to her.

'"You awake, Jack!" she cried with a nervous laugh. "Why, I thought that nothing could awake you."

'"Where have you been?" I asked, more sternly.

'"I don't wonder that you are surprised," said she, and I could see that her fingers were trembling as she undid the fastenings of her mantle. "Why, I never remember having done such a thing in my life before. The fact is that I felt as though I were choking and had a perfect longing for a breath of fresh air. I really think that I should have fainted if I had not gone out. I stood at the door for a few minutes, and now I am quite myself again."

'All the time that she was telling me this story she never once looked in my direction, and her voice was quite unlike her usual tones. It was evident to me that she was saying what was false. I said nothing in reply, but turned my face to the wall, sick at heart, with my mind filled with a thousand venomous doubts and suspicions. What was it that my wife was concealing from me? Where had she been during that strange expedition? I felt that I should have no peace until I knew, and yet I shrank from asking her again after once she had told me what was false. All the rest of the night I tossed and tumbled, framing theory after theory, each more unlikely than the last.

'I should have gone to the City that day, but I was too disturbed in my mind to be able to pay attention to business matters. My wife seemed to be as upset as myself, and I could see from the little questioning glances which she kept shooting at me that she understood that I disbelieved her statement, and that she was at her wit's end what to do. We hardly exchanged a word during breakfast, and immediately afterwards I went out for a walk that I might think the matter out in the fresh morning air.

'I went as far as the Crystal Palace, spent an hour in the grounds, and was back in Norbury by one o'clock. It happened that my way took me past the cottage, and I stopped for an instant to look at the windows and to see if I could catch a glimpse of the strange face which had looked out at me on the day before. As I stood there, imagine my surprise, Mr Holmes, when the door suddenly opened and my wife walked out.

'I was struck dumb with astonishment at the sight of her, but my emotions were nothing to those which showed themselves upon her face when our eyes met. She seemed for an instant to wish to shrink back inside the house again, and then, seeing how useless all concealment must be, she came forward, with a very white face and frightened eyes which belied the smile upon her lips.

'"Ah, Jack," she said, "I have just been in to see if I can be of any assistance to our new neighbours. Why do you look at me like that, Jack? You are not angry with me?"

'"So," said I, "this is where you went during the night."

'"What do you mean?" she cried.

'"You came here. I am sure of it. Who are these people that you should visit them at such an hour?"

'"I have not been here before."

'"How can you tell me what you know is false?" I cried. "Your very voice changes as you speak. When have I ever had a secret from you? I shall enter that cottage, and I shall probe the matter to the bottom."

'"No, no, Jack, for God's sake!" she gasped in uncontrollable emotion. Then, as I approached the door, she seized my sleeve and pulled me back with convulsive strength.

'"I implore you not to do this, Jack," she cried. "I swear that I will tell you everything some day, but nothing but misery can come of it if you enter that cottage." Then, as I tried to shake her off, she clung to me in a frenzy of entreaty.

'"Trust me, Jack!" she cried. "Trust me only this once. You will never have cause to regret it. You know that I would not have a secret from you if it were not for your own sake. Our whole lives are at stake in this. If you come home with me all will be well. If you force your way into that cottage all is over between us.'

'There was such earnestness, such despair, in her manner that face quite plainly, before I dropped off dozing by the fire. This may be a reason why Sophy, with her deaf-and-dumb child in her arms, seemed to stand silent by me all through my nap.

I was on the road, off the road, in all sorts of places, North and South and West and East, Winds liked best and winds liked least, Here and there and gone astray, Over the hills and far away, and still she stood silent by me, with her silent child in her arms. Even when I woke with a start, she seemed to vanish, as if she had stood by me in that very place only a single instant before.

I had started at a real sound, and the sound was on the steps of the cart. It was the light hurried tread of a child, coming clambering up. That tread of a child had once been so familiar to me, that for half a moment I believed I was a-going to see a little ghost.

But the touch of a real child was laid upon the outer handle of the door, and the handle turned, and the door opened a little way, and a real child peeped in. A bright little comely girl with large dark eyes.

Looking full at me, the tiny creature took off her mite of a straw hat, and a quantity of dark curls fell about her face. Then she opened her lips, and said in a pretty voice,

'Grandfather!'

'Ah, my God!' I cries out. 'She can speak!'

'Yes, dear grandfather. And I am to ask you whether there was ever any one that I remind you of?'

In a moment Sophy was round my neck, as well as the child, and her husband was a-wringing my hand with his face hid, and we all had to shake ourselves together before we could get over it. And when we did begin to get over it, and I saw the pretty child a-talking, pleased and quick and eager and busy, to her mother, in the signs that I had first taught her mother, the happy and yet pitying tears fell rolling down my face.

6

GEORGE SILVERMANS EXPLANATION

IT happened in this wise—

But, sitting with my pen in my hand looking at those words again, without descrying any hint in them of the words that should follow, it comes into my mind that they have an abrupt appearance. They may serve, however, if I let them remain, to suggest how very difficult I find it to begin to explain my explanation. An uncouth phrase: and yet I do not see my way to a better.

IT happened in THIS wise -

But, looking at those words, and comparing them with my former opening, I find they are the self-same words repeated. This is the more surprising to me, because I employ them in quite a new connection. For indeed I declare that my intention was to discard the commencement I first had in my thoughts, and to give the preference to another of an entirely different nature, dating my explanation from an anterior period of my life. I will make a third trial, without erasing this second failure, protesting that it is not my design to conceal any of my infirmities, whether they be of head or heart.

NOT as yet directly aiming at how it came to pass, I will come upon it by degrees. The natural manner, after all, for God knows that is how it came upon me.

My parents were in a miserable condition of life, and my

infant home was a cellar in Preston. I recollect the sound of father's Lancashire clogs on the street pavement above, as being different in my young hearing from the sound of all other clogs; and I recollect, that, when mother came down the cellar-steps, I used tremblingly to speculate on her feet having a good or an ill-tempered look,—on her knees,—on her waist,—until finally her face came into view, and settled the question. From this it will be seen that I was timid, and that the cellar-steps were steep, and that the doorway was very low.

Mother had the gripe and clutch of poverty upon her face, upon her figure, and not least of all upon her voice. Her sharp and high-pitched words were squeezed out of her, as by the compression of bony fingers on a leathern bag; and she had a way of rolling her eyes about and about the cellar, as she scolded, that was gaunt and hungry. Father, with his shoulders rounded, would sit quiet on a three-legged stool, looking at the empty grate, until she would pluck the stool from under him, and bid him go bring some money home. Then he would dismally ascend the steps; and I, holding my ragged shirt and trousers together with a hand (my only braces), would feint and dodge from mother's pursuing grasp at my hair.

A worldly little devil was mother's usual name for me. Whether I cried for that I was in the dark, or for that it was cold, or for that I was hungry, or whether I squeezed myself into a warm corner when there was a fire, or ate voraciously when there was food, she would still say, 'O, you worldly little devil!' And the sting of it was, that I quite well knew myself to be a worldly little devil. Worldly as to wanting to be housed and warmed, worldly as to wanting to be fed, worldly as to the greed with which I inwardly compared how much I got of those good things with how much father and mother got, when, rarely, those good things were going.

Sometimes they both went away seeking work; and then I would be locked up in the cellar for a day or two at a time. I was at my worldliest then. Left alone, I yielded myself up to a worldly yearning for enough of anything (except misery), and for the death of mother's father, who was a machine-maker at Birmingham, and on whose decease, I had heard mother say, she would come into a whole courtful of houses 'if she had her rights.' Worldly little devil, I would stand about, musingly fitting my cold bare feet into cracked bricks and crevices of the damp cellar-floor,—walking over my grandfather's body, so to speak, into the courtful of houses, and selling them for meat and drink, and clothes to wear.

At last a change came down into our cellar. The universal change came down even as low as that,—so will it mount to any height on which a human creature can perch,—and brought other changes with it.

We had a heap of I don't know what foul litter in the darkest corner, which we called 'the bed'. For three days mother lay upon it without getting up, and then began at times to laugh. If I had ever heard her laugh before, it had been so seldom that the strange sound frightened me. It frightened father too; and we took it by turns to give her water. Then she began to move her head from side to side, and sing. After that, she getting no better, father fell a-laughing and a-singing; and then there was only I to give them both water, and they both died.

WHEN I was lifted out of the cellar by two men, of whom one came peeping down alone first, and ran away and brought the other, I could hardly bear the light of the street. I was sitting in the road-way, blinking at it, and at a ring of people collected around me, but not close to me, when, true to my character of worldly little devil, I broke silence by saying, 'I am hungry and thirsty!'

'Does he know they are dead?' asked one of another.

'Do you know your father and mother are both dead of fever?' asked a third of me severely.

'I don't know what it is to be dead. I supposed it meant that, when the cup rattled against their teeth, and the water spilt over them. I am hungry and thirsty.' That was all I had to say about it.

The ring of people widened outward from the inner side as I looked around me; and I smelt vinegar, and what I know to be camphor, thrown in towards where I sat. Presently some one put a great vessel of smoking vinegar on the ground near me; and then they all looked at me in silent horror as I ate and drank of what was brought for me. I knew at the time they had a horror of me, but I couldn't help it.

I was still eating and drinking, and a murmur of discussion had begun to arise respecting what was to be done with me next, when I heard a cracked voice somewhere in the ring say, 'My name is Hawkyard, Mr Verity Hawkyard, of West Bromwich.' Then the ring split in one place; and a yellow-faced, peak-nosed gentleman, clad all in iron-gray to his gaiters, pressed forward with a policeman and another official of some sort. He came forward close to the vessel of smoking vinegar; from which he sprinkled himself carefully, and me copiously.

'He had a grandfather at Birmingham, this young boy, who is just dead too,' said Mr Hawkyard.

I turned my eyes upon the speaker, and said in a ravening manner, 'Where's his houses?'

'Hah! Horrible worldliness on the edge of the grave,' said Mr Hawkyard, casting more of the vinegar over me, as if to get my devil out of me. 'I have undertaken a slight—a very slight—trust in behalf of this boy; quite a voluntary trust: a matter of mere honour, if not of mere sentiment: still I have taken it upon myself, and it shall be (O, yes, it shall be!) discharged.'

The bystanders seemed to form an opinion of this gentleman much more favourable than their opinion of me.

'He shall be taught,' said Mr Hawkyard, '(O, yes, he shall be taught!) but what is to be done with him for the present? He may be infected. He may disseminate infection.' The ring widened considerably. 'What is to be done with him?'

He held some talk with the two officials. I could distinguish no word save 'Farm-house'. There was another sound several times repeated, which was wholly meaningless in my ears then, but which I knew afterwards to be 'Hoghton Towers'.

'Yes,' said Mr Hawkyard. 'I think that sounds promising; I think that sounds hopeful. And he can be put by himself in a ward, for a night or two, you say?'

It seemed to be the police-officer who had said so; for it was he who replied, Yes! It was he, too, who finally took me by the arm, and walked me before him through the streets, into a whitewashed room in a bare building, where I had a chair to sit in, a table to sit at, an iron bedstead and good mattress to lie upon, and a rug and blanket to cover me. Where I had enough to eat too, and was shown how to clean the tin porringer in which it was conveyed to me, until it was as good as a looking-glass. Here, likewise, I was put in a bath, and had new clothes brought to me; and my old rags were burnt, and I was camphored and vinegared and disinfected in a variety of ways.

When all this was done,—I don't know in how many days or how few, but it matters not,—Mr Hawkyard stepped in at the door, remaining close to it, and said, 'Go and stand against the opposite wall, George Silverman. As far off as you can. That'll do. How do you feel?'

I told him that I didn't feel cold, and didn't feel hungry, and didn't feel thirsty. That was the whole round of human feelings, as far as I knew, except the pain of being beaten.

'Well,' said he, 'you are going, George, to a healthy farm-house to be purified. Keep in the air there as much as you can. Live an out-of-door life there, until you are fetched away. You had better not say much—in fact, you had better be very careful not to say anything—about what your parents died of, or they might not like to take you in. Behave well, and I'll put you to school; O, yes! I'll put you to school, though I'm not obligated to do it. I am a servant of the Lord, George; and I have been a good servant to him, I have, these five-and-thirty years. The Lord has had a good servant in me, and he knows it.'

What I then supposed him to mean by this, I cannot imagine. As little do I know when I began to comprehend that he was a prominent member of some obscure denomination or congregation, every member of which held forth to the rest when so inclined, and among whom he was called Brother Hawkyard. It was enough for me to know, on that day in the ward, that the farmer's cart was waiting for me at the street corner. I was not slow to get into it; for it was the first ride I ever had in my life.

It made me sleepy, and I slept.

First, I stared at Preston streets as long as they lasted; and, meanwhile, I may have had some small dumb wondering within me whereabouts our cellar was; but I doubt it. Such a worldly little devil was I, that I took no thought who would bury father and mother, or where they would be buried, or when. The question whether the eating and drinking by day, and the covering by night, would be as good at the farm-house as at the ward superseded those questions.

The jolting of the cart on a loose stony road awoke me; and I found that we were mounting a steep hill, where the road was a rutty by-road through a field. And so, by fragments of an ancient terrace, and by some rugged outbuildings that had once been fortified, and passing under a ruined gateway we came to the old farm-house in the thick stone wall outside the old quadrangle of Hoghton Towers which I looked at like a stupid savage, seeing no speciality in, seeing no antiquity in; assuming all farm-houses to resemble it; assigning the decay I noticed to the one potent cause of all ruin that I knew,—poverty; eyeing the pigeons in their flights, the cattle in their stalls, the ducks in the pond, and the fowls pecking about the yard, with a hungry hope that plenty of them might be killed for dinner while I stayed there; wondering whether the scrubbed dairy vessels, drying in the sunlight, could be goodly porringers out of which the master ate his belly-filling food, and which he polished when he had done, according to my ward experience; shrinkingly doubtful whether the shadows, passing over that airy height on the bright spring day, were not something in the nature of frowns,—sordid, afraid, unadmiring,—a small brute to shudder at.

To that time I had never had the faintest impression of duty. I had had no knowledge whatever that there was anything lovely in this life. When I had occasionally slunk up the cellar-steps into the street, and glared in at shop-windows, I had done so with no higher feelings than we may suppose to animate a mangy young dog or wolf-cub. It is equally the fact that I had never been alone, in the sense of holding unselfish converse with myself. I had been solitary often enough, but nothing better.

Such was my condition when I sat down to my dinner that day, in the kitchen of the old farm-house. Such was my condition when I lay on my bed in the old farm-house that night, stretched out opposite the narrow mullioned window, in the cold light of the moon, like a young vampire.

WHAT do I know of Hoghton Towers? Very little; for I have been gratefully unwilling to disturb my first impressions. A house, centuries old, on high ground a mile or so removed from the road between Preston and Blackburn, where the first James of England, in his hurry to make money by making baronets, perhaps made some of those remunerative dignitaries. A house, centuries old, deserted and falling to pieces, its woods and gardens long since grass-land or ploughed up, the Rivers Ribble and Darwen glancing below it, and a vague haze of smoke, against which not even the supernatural prescience of the first Stuart could foresee a counter-blast, hinting at steam-power, powerful in two distances.

What did I know then of Hoghton Towers? When I first peeped in at the gate of the lifeless quadrangle, and started from the mouldering statue becoming visible to me like its guardian ghost; when I stole round by the back of the farm-house, and got in among the ancient rooms, many of them with their floors and ceilings falling, the beams and rafters hanging dangerously down, the plaster dropping as I trod, the oaken panels stripped away, the windows half walled up, half broken; when I discovered a gallery commanding the old kitchen, and looked down between balustrades upon a massive old table and benches, fearing to see I know not what dead-alive creatures come in and seat themselves, and look up with I know not what dreadful eyes, or lack of eyes, at me; when all over the house I was awed by gaps and chinks where the sky stared sorrowfully at me, where the birds passed, and the ivy rustled, and the stains of winter weather blotched the rotten floors; when down at the bottom of dark pits of staircase, into which the stairs had sunk, green leaves trembled, butterflies fluttered, and bees hummed in and out through the broken doorways; when encircling the whole ruin were sweet scents, and sights of fresh green growth, and ever-renewing life, that I had never dreamed of,—I say, when I passed into such clouded perception of these things as my dark soul could compass, what did I know then of Hoghton Towers?

I have written that the sky stared sorrowfully at me. Therein have I anticipated the answer. I knew that all these things looked sorrowfully at me; that they seemed to sigh or whisper, not without pity for me, 'Alas! poor worldly little devil!'

There were two or three rats at the bottom of one of the smaller pits of broken staircase when I craned over and looked in. They were scuffling for some prey that was there; and, when they started and hid themselves close together in the dark, I thought of the old life (it had grown old already) in the cellar.

How not to be this worldly little devil? how not to have a repugnance towards myself as I had towards the rats? I hid in a corner of one of the smaller chambers, frightened at myself, and crying (it was the first time I had ever cried for any cause not purely physical), and I tried to think about it. One of the farm-ploughs came into my range of view just then; and it seemed to help me as it went on with its two horses up and down the field so peacefully and quietly.

There was a girl of about my own age in the farm-house family, and she sat opposite to me at the narrow table at meal times. It had come into my mind, at our first dinner, that she might take the fever from me. The thought had not disquieted me then. I had only speculated how she would look under the altered circumstances, and whether she would die. But it came into my mind now, that I might try to prevent her taking the fever by keeping away from her. I knew I should have but scrambling board if I did; so much the less worldly and less devilish the deed would be, I thought.

From that hour, I withdrew myself at early morning into secret corners of the ruined house, and remained hidden there until she went to bed. At first, when meals were ready, I used to hear them calling me; and then my resolution weakened. But I strengthened it again by going farther off into the ruin, and getting out of hearing. I often watched for her at the dim windows; and, when I saw that she was fresh and rosy, felt much happier.

Out of this holding her in my thoughts, to the humanising of myself, I suppose some childish love arose within me.

I felt, in some sort, dignified by the pride of protecting her,—by the pride of making the sacrifice for her. As my heart swelled with that new feeling, it insensibly softened about mother and father. It seemed to have been frozen before, and now to be thawed. The old ruin and all the lovely things that haunted it were not sorrowful for me only, but sorrowful for mother and father as well. Therefore did I cry again, and often too.

The farm-house family conceived me to be of a morose temper, and were very short with me; though they never stinted me in such broken fare as was to be got out of regular hours. One night when I lifted the kitchen latch at my usual time, Sylvia (that was her pretty name) had but just gone out of the room. Seeing her ascending the opposite stairs, I stood still at the door. She had heard the clink of the latch, and looked round.

'George,' she called to me in a pleased voice, 'to-morrow is my birthday; and we are to have a fiddler, and there's a party of boys and girls coming in a cart, and we shall dance. I invite you. Be sociable for once, George.'

'I am very sorry, miss,' I answered; 'but I—but, no; I can't come.'

'You are a disagreeable, ill-humoured lad,' she returned disdainfully; 'and I ought not to have asked you. I shall never speak to you again.'

As I stood with my eyes fixed on the fire, after she was gone, I felt that the farmer bent his brows upon me.

'Eh, lad!' said he; 'Sylvy's right. You're as moody and broody a lad as never I set eyes on yet.'

I tried to assure him that I meant no harm; but he only said coldly, 'Maybe not, maybe not! There, get thy supper, get thy supper; and then thou canst sulk to thy heart's content again.'

Ah! if they could have seen me next day, in the ruin, watching for the arrival of the cart full of merry young guests; if they could have seen me at night, gliding out from behind the ghostly statue, listening to the music and the fall of dancing feet, and watching the lighted farm-house windows from the quadrangle when all the ruin was dark; if they could have read my heart, as I crept up to bed by the back way, comforting myself with the reflection, 'They will take no hurt from me,'—they would not have thought mine a morose or an unsocial nature.

It was in these ways that I began to form a shy disposition; to be of a timidly silent character under misconstruction; to have an inexpressible, perhaps a morbid, dread of ever being sordid or worldly. It was in these ways that my nature came to shape itself to such a mould, even before it was affected by the influences of the studious and retired life of a poor scholar.

BROTHER HAWKYARD (as he insisted on my calling him) put me to school, and told me to work my way. 'You are all right, George,' he said. 'I have been the best servant the Lord has had in his service for this five-and-thirty year (O, I have!); and he knows the value of such a servant as I have been to him (O, yes, he does!); and he'll prosper your schooling as a part of my reward. That's what HE'll do, George. He'll do it for me.'

From the first I could not like this familiar knowledge of the ways of the sublime, inscrutable Almighty, on Brother Hawkyard's part. As I grew a little wiser, and still a little wiser, I liked it less and less.

His manner, too, of confirming himself in a parenthesis,—as if, knowing himself, he doubted his own word,—I found distasteful. I cannot tell how much these dislikes cost me; for I had a dread that they were worldly.

As time went on, I became a Foundation-boy on a good foundation, and I cost Brother Hawkyard nothing. When I had worked my way so far, I worked yet harder, in the hope of ultimately getting a presentation to college and a fellowship. My health has never been strong (some vapour from the Preston cellar cleaves to me, I think); and what with much work and some weakness, I came again to be regarded—that is, by my fellow students—as unsocial.

All through my time as a foundation boy, I was within a few miles of Brother Hawkyard's congregation; and whenever I was what we called a leave-boy on a Sunday, I went over there at his desire. Before the knowledge became forced upon me that outside their place of meeting these brothers and sisters were no better than the rest of the human family, but on the whole were, to put the case mildly, as bad as most, in respect of giving short weight in their shops, and not speaking the truth,—I say, before this knowledge became forced upon me, their prolix addresses, their inordinate conceit, their daring ignorance, their investment of the Supreme Ruler of heaven and earth with their own miserable meannesses and littlenesses, greatly shocked me. Still, as their term for the frame of mind that could not perceive them to be in an exalted state of grace was the 'worldly' state, I did for a time suffer tortures under my inquiries of myself whether that young worldly-devilish spirit of mine could secretly be lingering at the bottom of my non-appreciation.

Brother Hawkyard was the popular expounder in this assembly, and generally occupied the platform (there was a little platform with a table on it, in lieu of a pulpit) first, on a Sunday afternoon. He was by trade a drysalter. Brother Gimblet, an elderly man with a crabbed face, a large dog's-eared shirt-collar, and a spotted blue neckerchief reaching up behind to the crown of his head, was also a drysalter and an expounder. Brother Gimblet professed the greatest admiration for Brother Hawkyard, but (I had thought more than once) bore him a jealous grudge.

Let whosoever may peruse these lines kindly take the pains here to read twice my solemn pledge, that what I write of the language and customs of the congregation in question I write scrupulously, literally, exactly, from the life and the truth.

On the first Sunday after I had won what I had so long tried for, and when it was certain that I was going up to college, Brother Hawkyard concluded a long exhortation thus:

'Well, my friends and fellow-sinners, now I told you when I began, that I didn't know a word of what I was going to say to you (and no, I did not!), but that it was all one to me, because I knew the Lord would put into my mouth the words I wanted.'

('That's it!' from Brother Gimblet.)

'And he did put into my mouth the words I wanted.'

('So he did!' from Brother Gimblet.)

'And why?'

('Ah, let's have that!' from Brother Gimblet.)

'Because I have been his faithful servant for five-and-thirty years, and because he knows it. For five-and-thirty years! And he knows it, mind you! I got those words that I wanted on account of my wages.

I got 'em from the Lord, my fellow-sinners. Down! I said, 'Here's a heap of wages due; let us have something down, on account.' And I got it down, and I paid it over to you; and you won't wrap it up in a napkin, nor yet in a towel, nor yet pocketankercher, but you'll put it out at good interest. Very well. Now, my brothers and sisters and fellow-sinners, I am going to conclude with a question, and I'll make it so plain (with the help of the Lord, after five-and-thirty years, I should rather hope!) as that the Devil shall not be able to confuse it in your heads,—which he would be overjoyed to do.'

('Just his way. Crafty old blackguard!' from Brother Gimblet.)

'And the question is this, Are the angels learned?'

('Not they. Not a bit on it!' from Brother Gimblet, with the greatest confidence.)

'Not they. And where's the proof? sent ready-made by the hand of the Lord. Why, there's one among us here now, that has got all the learning that can be crammed into him. I got him all the learning that could be crammed into him. His grandfather' (this I had never heard before) 'was a brother of ours. He was Brother Parksop. That's what he was. Parksop; Brother Parksop. His worldly name was Parksop, and he was a brother of this brotherhood. Then wasn't he Brother Parksop?'

('Must be. Couldn't help hisself!' from Brother Gimblet.)

'Well, he left that one now here present among us to the care of a brother-sinner of his (and that brother-sinner, mind you, was a sinner of a bigger size in his time than any of you; praise the Lord!), Brother Hawkyard. Me. I got him without fee or reward,—

without a morsel of myrrh, or frankincense, nor yet amber, letting alone the honeycomb,—all the learning that could be crammed into him. Has it brought him into our temple, in the spirit? No. Have we had any ignorant brothers and sisters that didn't know round O from crooked S, come in among us meanwhile? Many. Then the angels are NOT learned; then they don't so much as know their alphabet. And now, my friends and fellow-sinners, having brought it to that, perhaps some brother present—perhaps you, Brother Gimblet—will pray a bit for us?'

Brother Gimblet undertook the sacred function, after having drawn his sleeve across his mouth, and muttered, 'Well! I don't know as I see my way to hitting any of you quite in the right place neither.' He said this with a dark smile, and then began to bellow. What we were specially to be preserved from, according to his solicitations, was, despoilment of the orphan, suppression of testamentary intentions on the part of a father or (say) grandfather, appropriation of the orphan's house-property, feigning to give in charity to the wronged one from whom we withheld his due; and that class of sins. He ended with the petition, 'Give us peace!' which, speaking for myself, was very much needed after twenty minutes of his bellowing.

Even though I had not seen him when he rose from his knees, steaming with perspiration, glance at Brother Hawkyard, and even though I had not heard Brother Hawkyard's tone of congratulating him on the vigour with which he had roared, I should have detected a malicious application in this prayer.

Unformed suspicions to a similar effect had sometimes passed through my mind in my earlier school days, and had always caused me great distress; for they were worldly in their nature, and wide, very wide, of the spirit that had drawn me from Sylvia. They were sordid suspicions, without a shadow of proof. They were worthy to have originated in the unwholesome cellar. They were not only without proof, but against proof; for was I not myself a living proof of what Brother Hawkyard had done? and without him, how should I ever have seen the sky look sorrowfully down upon that wretched boy at Hoghton Towers?

Although the dread of a relapse into a stage of savage selfishness was less strong upon me as I approached manhood, and could act in an increased degree for myself, yet I was always on my guard against any tendency to such relapse. After getting these suspicions under my feet, I had been troubled by not being able to like Brother Hawkyard's manner, or his professed religion. So it came about, that, as I walked back that Sunday evening, I thought it would be an act of reparation for any such injury my struggling thoughts had unwillingly done him, if I wrote, and placed in his hands, before going to college, a full acknowledgment of his goodness to me, and an ample tribute of thanks. It might serve as an implied vindication of him against any dark scandal from a rival brother and expounder, or from any other quarter.

Accordingly, I wrote the document with much care. I may add with much feeling too; for it affected me as I went on. Having no set studies to pursue, in the brief interval between leaving the Foundation and going to Cambridge, I determined to walk out to his place of business, and give it into his own hands.

It was a winter afternoon, when I tapped at the door of his little counting-house, which was at the farther end of his long, low shop. As I did so (having entered by the back yard, where casks and boxes were taken in, and where there was the inscription, 'Private way to the counting-house'), a shopman called to me from the counter that he was engaged.

'Brother Gimblet' (said the shopman, who was one of the brotherhood) 'is with him.'

I thought this all the better for my purpose, and made bold to tap again. They were talking in a low tone, and money was passing; for I heard it being counted out.

'Who is it?' asked Brother Hawkyard, sharply.

'George Silverman,' I answered, holding the door open. 'May I come in?'

Both brothers seemed so astounded to see me that I felt shyer than usual. But they looked quite cadaverous in the early gaslight, and perhaps that accidental circumstance exaggerated the expression of their faces.

'What is the matter?' asked Brother Hawkyard.

'Ay! what is the matter?' asked Brother Gimblet.

'Nothing at all,' I said, diffidently producing my document: 'I am only the bearer of a letter from myself.'

'From yourself, George?' cried Brother Hawkyard.

'And to you,' said I.

'And to me, George?'

He turned paler, and opened it hurriedly; but looking over it, and seeing generally what it was, became less hurried, recovered his colour, and said, 'Praise the Lord!'

'That's it!' cried Brother Gimblet. 'Well put! Amen.'

Brother Hawkyard then said, in a livelier strain, 'You must know, George, that Brother Gimblet and I are going to make our two businesses one. We are going into partnership. We are settling it now. Brother Gimblet is to take one clear half of the profits (O, yes! he shall have it; he shall have it to the last farthing).

'D.V.!' said Brother Gimblet, with his right fist firmly clinched on his right leg.

'There is no objection,' pursued Brother Hawkyard, 'to my reading this aloud, George?'

As it was what I expressly desired should be done, after yesterday's prayer, I more than readily begged him to read it aloud. He did so; and Brother Gimblet listened with a crabbed smile.

'It was in a good hour that I came here,' he said, wrinkling up his eyes. 'It was in a good hour, likewise, that I was moved yesterday to depict for the terror of evil-doers a character the direct opposite of Brother Hawkyard's. But it was the Lord that done it: I felt him at it while I was perspiring.'

After that it was proposed by both of them that I should attend the congregation once more before my final departure. What my shy reserve would undergo, from being expressly preached at and prayed at, I knew beforehand. But I reflected that it would be for the last time, and that it might add to the weight of my letter. It was well known to the brothers and sisters that there was no place taken for me in THEIR paradise; and if I showed this last token of deference to Brother Hawkyard, notoriously in despite of my own sinful inclinations, it might go some little way in aid of my statement that he had been good to me, and that I was grateful to him. Merely stipulating, therefore, that no express endeavour should be made for my conversion,—which would involve the rolling of several brothers and sisters on the floor, declaring that they felt all their sins in a heap on their left side, weighing so many pounds avoirdupois, as I knew from what I had seen of those repulsive mysteries,—I promised.

Since the reading of my letter, Brother Gimblet had been at intervals wiping one eye with an end of his spotted blue neckerchief, and grinning to himself. It was, however, a habit that brother had, to grin in an ugly manner even when expounding. I call to mind a delighted snarl with which he used to detail from the platform the torments reserved for the wicked (meaning all human creation except the brotherhood), as being remarkably hideous.

I left the two to settle their articles of partnership, and count money; and I never saw them again but on the following Sunday. Brother Hawkyard died within two or three years, leaving all he possessed to Brother Gimblet, in virtue of a will dated (as I have been told) that very day.

Now I was so far at rest with myself, when Sunday came, knowing that I had conquered my own mistrust, and righted Brother Hawkyard in the jaundiced vision of a rival, that I went, even to that coarse chapel, in a less sensitive state than usual. How could I foresee that the delicate, perhaps the diseased, corner of my mind, where I winced and shrunk when it was touched, or was even approached, would be handled as the theme of the whole proceedings?

On this occasion it was assigned to Brother Hawkyard to pray, and to Brother Gimblet to preach. The prayer was to open the ceremonies; the discourse was to come next. Brothers Hawkyard and Gimblet were both on the platform; Brother Hawkyard on his knees at the table, unmusically ready to pray; Brother Gimblet sitting against the wall, grinningly ready to preach.

'Let us offer up the sacrifice of prayer, my brothers and sisters and fellow-sinners.' Yes; but it was I who was the sacrifice.

It was our poor, sinful, worldly-minded brother here present who was wrestled for. The now-opening career of this our unawakened brother might lead to his becoming a minister of what was called 'the church.' That was what HE looked to. The church. Not the chapel, Lord. The church. No rectors, no vicars, no archdeacons, no bishops, no archbishops, in the chapel, but, O Lord! many such in the church. Protect our sinful brother from his love of lucre. Cleanse from our unawakened brother's breast his sin of worldly-mindedness. The prayer said infinitely more in words, but nothing more to any intelligible effect.

Then Brother Gimblet came forward, and took (as I knew he would) the text, 'My kingdom is not of this world.' Ah! but whose was, my fellow-sinners? Whose? Why, our brother's here present was. The only kingdom he had an idea of was of this world. ('That's it!' from several of the congregation.) What did the woman do when she lost the piece of money? Went and looked for it. What should our brother do when he lost his way? ('Go and look for it,' from a sister.) Go and look for it, true. But must he look for it in the right direction, or in the wrong? ('In the right,' from a brother.) There spake the prophets! He must look for it in the right direction, or he couldn't find it. But he had turned his back upon the right direction, and he wouldn't find it. Now, my fellow-sinners, to show you the difference betwixt worldly-mindedness and unworldly-mindedness, betwixt kingdoms not of this world and kingdoms of this world, here was a letter wrote by even our worldly-minded brother unto Brother Hawkyard. Judge, from hearing of it read, whether Brother Hawkyard was the faithful steward that the Lord had in his mind only t'other day, when, in this very place, he drew you the picter of the unfaithful one; for it was him that done it, not me. Don't doubt that!

Brother Gimblet then groaned and bellowed his way through my composition, and subsequently through an hour. The service closed with a hymn, in which the brothers unanimously roared, and the sisters unanimously shrieked at me, That I by wiles of worldly gain was mocked, and they on waters of sweet love were rocked; that I with mammon struggled in the dark, while they were floating in a second ark.

I went out from all this with an aching heart and a weary spirit: not because I was quite so weak as to consider these narrow creatures interpreters of the Divine Majesty and Wisdom, but because I was weak enough to feel as though it were my hard fortune to be misrepresented and misunderstood, when I most tried to subdue any risings of mere worldliness within me, and when I most hoped that, by dint of trying earnestly, I had succeeded.

My timidity and my obscurity occasioned me to live a secluded life at college, and to be little known. No relative ever came to visit me, for I had no relative. No intimate friends broke in upon my studies, for I made no intimate friends. I supported myself on my scholarship, and read much. My college time was otherwise not so very different from my time at Hoghton Towers.

Knowing myself to be unfit for the noisier stir of social existence, but believing myself qualified to do my duty in a moderate, though earnest way, if I could obtain some small preferment in the Church, I applied my mind to the clerical profession. In due sequence I took orders, was ordained, and began to look about me for employment. I must observe that I had taken a good degree, that I had succeeded in winning a good fellowship, and that my means were ample for my retired way of life. By this time I had read with several young men; and the occupation increased my income, while it was highly interesting to me. I once accidentally overheard our greatest don say, to my boundless joy, 'That he heard it reported of Silverman that his gift of quiet explanation, his patience, his amiable temper, and his conscientiousness made him the best of coaches.' May my 'gift of quiet explanation' come more seasonably and powerfully to my aid in this present explanation than I think it will!

It may be in a certain degree owing to the situation of my college rooms (in a corner where the daylight was sobered), but it is in a much larger degree referable to the state of my own mind, that I seem to myself, on looking back to this time of my life, to have been always in the peaceful shade. I can see others in the sunlight; I can see our boats' crews and our athletic young men on the glistening water, or speckled with the moving lights of sunlit leaves; but I myself am always in the shadow looking on. Not unsympathetically,—God forbid!—but looking on alone, much as I looked at Sylvia from the shadows of the ruined house, or looked at the red gleam shining through the farmer's windows, and listened to the fall of dancing feet, when all the ruin was dark that night in the quadrangle.

I now come to the reason of my quoting that laudation of myself above given. Without such reason, to repeat it would have been mere boastfulness.

Among those who had read with me was Mr Fareway, second son of Lady Fareway, widow of Sir Gaston Fareway, baronet. This young gentleman's abilities were much above the average; but he came of a rich family, and was idle and luxurious. He presented himself to me too late, and afterwards came to me too irregularly, to admit of my being of much service to him. In the end, I considered it my duty to dissuade him from going up for an examination which he could never pass; and he left college without a degree. After his departure, Lady Fareway wrote to me, representing the justice of my returning half my fee, as I had been of so little use to her son. Within my knowledge a similar demand had not been made in any other case; and I most freely admit that the justice of it had not occurred to me until it was pointed out. But I at once perceived it, yielded to it, and returned the money -

Mr Fareway had been gone two years or more, and I had forgotten him, when he one day walked into my rooms as I was sitting at my books.

Said he, after the usual salutations had passed, 'Mr Silverman, my mother is in town here, at the hotel, and wishes me to present you to her.'

I was not comfortable with strangers, and I dare say I betrayed that I was a little nervous or unwilling. 'For,' said he, without my having spoken, 'I think the interview may tend to the advancement of your prospects.'

It put me to the blush to think that I should be tempted by a worldly reason, and I rose immediately.

Said Mr Fareway, as we went along, 'Are you a good hand at business?'

'I think not,' said I.

Said Mr Fareway then, 'My mother is.'

'Truly?' said I.

'Yes, my mother is what is usually called a managing woman. Doesn't make a bad thing, for instance, even out of the spendthrift habits of my eldest brother abroad. In short, a managing woman. This is in confidence.'

He had never spoken to me in confidence, and I was surprised by his doing so. I said I should respect his confidence, of course, and said no more on the delicate subject. We had but a little way to walk, and I was soon in his mother's company. He presented me, shook hands with me, and left us two (as he said) to business.

I saw in my Lady Fareway a handsome, well-preserved lady of somewhat large stature, with a steady glare in her great round dark eyes that embarrassed me.

Said my lady, 'I have heard from my son, Mr Silverman, that you would be glad of some preferment in the church.' I gave my lady to understand that was so.

'I don't know whether you are aware,' my lady proceeded, 'that we have a presentation to a living? I say WE have; but, in point of fact, I have.'

I gave my lady to understand that I had not been aware of this.

Said my lady, 'So it is: indeed I have two presentations,—one to two hundred a year, one to six. Both livings are in our county,—North Devonshire,—as you probably know. The first is vacant. Would you like it?'

What with my lady's eyes, and what with the suddenness of this proposed gift, I was much confused.

'I am sorry it is not the larger presentation,' said my lady, rather coldly; 'though I will not, Mr Silverman, pay you the bad compliment of supposing that YOU are, because that would be mercenary,—and mercenary I am persuaded you are not.'

Said I, with my utmost earnestness, 'Thank you, Lady Fareway, thank you, thank you! I should be deeply hurt if I thought I bore the character.'

'Naturally,' said my lady. 'Always detestable, but particularly in a clergyman. You have not said whether you will like the living?'

With apologies for my remissness or indistinctness, I assured my lady that I accepted it most readily and gratefully. I added that I hoped she would not estimate my appreciation of the generosity of her choice by my flow of words; for I was not a ready man in that respect when taken by surprise or touched at heart.

'The affair is concluded,' said my lady; 'concluded. You

will find the duties very light, Mr Silverman. Charming house; charming little garden, orchard, and all that. You will be able to take pupils. By the bye! No: I will return to the word afterwards. What was I going to mention, when it put me out?'

My lady stared at me, as if I knew. And I didn't know. And that perplexed me afresh.

Said my lady, after some consideration, 'O, of course, how very dull of me! The last incumbent,—least mercenary man I ever saw,—in consideration of the duties being so light and the house so delicious, couldn't rest, he said, unless I permitted him to help me with my correspondence, accounts, and various little things of that kind; nothing in themselves, but which it worries a lady to cope with. Would Mr Silverman also like to? Or shall I?'

I hastened to say that my poor help would be always at her ladyship's service.

'I am absolutely blessed,' said my lady, casting up her eyes (and so taking them off me for one moment), 'in having to do with gentlemen who cannot endure an approach to the idea of being mercenary!' She shivered at the word. 'And now as to the pupil.'

'The?' I was quite at a loss.

'Mr Silverman, you have no idea what she is. She is,' said my lady, laying her touch upon my coat-sleeve, 'I do verily believe, the most extraordinary girl in this world. Already knows more Greek and Latin than Lady Jane Grey. And taught herself! Has not yet, remember, derived a moment's advantage from Mr Silverman's classical acquirements. To say nothing of mathematics, which she is bent upon becoming versed in, and in which (as I hear from my son and others) Mr Silverman's reputation is so deservedly high!'

Under my lady's eyes I must have lost the clue, I felt persuaded; and yet I did not know where I could have dropped it.

'Adelina,' said my lady, 'is my only daughter. If I did not feel quite convinced that I am not blinded by a mother's partiality; unless I was absolutely sure that when you know her, Mr Silverman, you will esteem it a high and unusual privilege to direct her studies,—I should introduce a mercenary element into this conversation, and ask you on what terms—'

I entreated my lady to go no further. My lady saw that I was troubled, and did me the honour to comply with my request.

Everything in mental acquisition that her brother might have been, if he would, and everything in all gracious charms and admirable qualities that no one but herself could be,—this was Adelina.

I will not expatiate upon her beauty; I will not expatiate upon her intelligence, her quickness of perception, her powers of memory, her sweet consideration, from the first moment, for the slow-paced tutor who ministered to her wonderful gifts. I was thirty then; I am over sixty now, she is ever present to me in these hours as she was in those, bright and beautiful and young, wise and fanciful and good.

When I discovered that I loved her, how can I say? In the first day? In the first week? In the first month? Impossible to trace. If I be (as I am) unable to represent to myself any previous period of my life as quite separable from her attracting power, how can I answer for this one detail?

Whensoever I made the discovery, it laid a heavy burden on me. And yet, comparing it with the far heavier burden that I afterwards took up, it does not seem to me now to have been very hard to bear. In the knowledge that I did love her, and that I should love her while my life lasted, and that I was ever to hide my secret deep in my own breast, and she was never to find it, there was a kind of sustaining joy or pride, or comfort, mingled with my pain.

But later on,—say, a year later on,—when I made another discovery, then indeed my suffering and my struggle were strong. That other discovery was-

These words will never see the light, if ever, until my heart is dust; until her bright spirit has returned to the regions of which, when imprisoned here, it surely retained some unusual glimpse of remembrance; until all the pulses that ever beat around us shall have long been quiet; until all the fruits of all the tiny victories and defeats achieved in our little breasts shall have withered away. That discovery was that she loved me.

She may have enhanced my knowledge, and loved me for that; she may have over-valued my discharge of duty to her, and loved me for that; she may have refined upon a playful compassion which she would sometimes show for what she called my want of wisdom, according to the light of the world's dark lanterns, and loved me for that; she may—she must—have confused the borrowed light of what I had only learned, with its brightness in its pure, original rays; but she loved me at that time, and she made me know it.

Pride of family and pride of wealth put me as far off from her in my lady's eyes as if I had been some domesticated creature of another kind. But they could not put me farther from her than I put myself when I set my merits against hers. More than that. They could not put me, by millions of fathoms, half so low beneath her as I put myself when in imagination I took advantage of her noble trustfulness, took the fortune that I knew she must possess in her own right, and left her to find herself, in the zenith of her beauty and genius, bound to poor rusty, plodding me.

No! Worldliness should not enter here at any cost. If I had tried to keep it out of other ground, how much harder was I bound to try to keep it out from this sacred place!

But there was something daring in her broad, generous character, that demanded at so delicate a crisis to be delicately and patiently addressed. And many and many a bitter night (O, I found I could cry for reasons not purely physical, at this pass of my life!) I took my course.

My lady had, in our first interview, unconsciously overstated the accommodation of my pretty house. There was room in it for only one pupil. He was a young gentleman near coming of age, very well connected, but what is called a poor relation. His parents were dead. The charges of his living and reading with me were defrayed by an uncle; and he and I were to do our utmost together for three years towards qualifying him to make his way. At this time he had entered into his second year with me. He was well-looking, clever, energetic, enthusiastic, bold, in the best sense of the term, a thorough young Anglo-Saxon.

I resolved to bring these two together.

SAID I, one night, when I had conquered myself, 'Mr Granville,'—Mr Granville Wharton his name was,—'I doubt if you have ever yet so much as seen Miss Fareway.'

'Well, sir,' returned he, laughing, 'you see her so much yourself, that you hardly leave another fellow a chance of seeing her.'

'I am her tutor, you know,' said I.

And there the subject dropped for that time. But I so contrived as that they should come together shortly afterwards. I had previously so contrived as to keep them asunder; for while I loved her,—I mean before I had determined on my sacrifice,—a lurking jealousy of Mr Granville lay within my unworthy breast.

It was quite an ordinary interview in the Fareway Park but they talked easily together for some time: like takes to like, and they had many points of resemblance. Said Mr Granville to me, when he and I sat at our supper that night, 'Miss Fareway is remarkably beautiful, sir, remarkably engaging. Don't you think so?' 'I think so,' said I. And I stole a glance at him, and saw that he had reddened and was thoughtful.

I remember it most vividly, because the mixed feeling of grave pleasure and acute pain that the slight circumstance caused me was the first of a long, long series of such mixed impressions under which my hair turned slowly gray.

I had not much need to feign to be subdued; but I counterfeited to be older than I was in all respects (Heaven knows! my heart being all too young the while), and feigned to be more of a recluse and bookworm than I had really become, and gradually set up more and more of a fatherly manner towards Adelina. Likewise I made my tuition less imaginative than before; separated myself from my poets and philosophers; was careful to present them in their own light, and me, their lowly servant, in my own shade. Moreover, in the matter of apparel I was equally mindful; not that I had ever been dapper that way; but that I was slovenly now.

As I depressed myself with one hand, so did I labour to raise Mr Granville with the other; directing his attention to such subjects as I too well knew interested her, and fashioning him (do not deride or misconstrue the expression, unknown reader of this writing; for I have suffered!) into a greater resemblance to myself in my solitary one strong aspect. And gradually, gradually, as I saw him take more and more to these thrown-out lures of mine, then did I come to know better and better that love was drawing him on, and was drawing her from me.

So passed more than another year; every day a year in its number of my mixed impressions of grave pleasure and acute pain; and then these two, being of age and free to act legally for themselves, came before me hand in hand (my hair being now quite white), and entreated me that I would unite them together. 'And indeed, dear tutor,' said Adelina, 'it is but consistent in you that you should do this thing for us, seeing that we should never have spoken together that first time but for you, and that but for you we could never have met so often afterwards.' The whole of which was literally true; for I had availed myself of my many business attendances on, and conferences with, my lady, to take Mr Granville to the house, and leave him in the outer room with Adelina.

I knew that my lady would object to such a marriage for her daughter, or to any marriage that was other than an exchange of her for stipulated lands, goods, and moneys. But looking on the two, and seeing with full eyes that they were both young and beautiful; and knowing that they were alike in the tastes and acquirements that will outlive youth and beauty; and considering that Adelina had a fortune now, in her own keeping; and considering further that Mr Granville, though for the present poor, was of a good family that had never lived in a cellar in Preston; and believing that their love would endure, neither having any great discrepancy to find out in the other,—I told them of my readiness to do this thing which Adelina asked of her dear tutor, and to send them forth, husband and wife, into the shining world with golden gates that awaited them.

It was on a summer morning that I rose before the sun to compose myself for the crowning of my work with this end; and my dwelling being near to the sea, I walked down to the rocks on the shore, in order that I might behold the sun in his majesty.

The tranquillity upon the deep, and on the firmament, the orderly withdrawal of the stars, the calm promise of coming day, the rosy suffusion of the sky and waters, the ineffable splendour that then burst forth, attuned my mind afresh after the discords of the night.

Methought that all I looked on said to me, and that all I heard in the sea and in the air said to me, 'Be comforted, mortal, that thy life is so short. Our preparation for what is to follow has endured, and shall endure, for unimaginable ages.'

I married them. I knew that my hand was cold when I placed it on their hands clasped together; but the words with which I had to accompany the action I could say without faltering, and I was at peace.

They being well away from my house and from the place after our simple breakfast, the time was come when I must do what I had pledged myself to them that I would do,—break the intelligence to my lady.

I went up to the house, and found my lady in her ordinary

business-room. She happened to have an unusual amount of commissions to intrust to me that day; and she had filled my hands with papers before I could originate a word.

'My lady,' I then began, as I stood beside her table.

'Why, what's the matter?' she said quickly, looking up.

'Not much, I would fain hope, after you shall have prepared yourself, and considered a little.'

'Prepared myself; and considered a little! You appear to have prepared YOURSELF but indifferently, anyhow, Mr Silverman.' This mighty scornfully, as I experienced my usual embarrassment under her stare.

Said I, in self-extenuation once for all, 'Lady Fareway, I have but to say for myself that I have tried to do my duty.'

'For yourself?' repeated my lady. 'Then there are others concerned, I see. Who are they?'

I was about to answer, when she made towards the bell with a dart that stopped me, and said, 'Why, where is Adelina?'

'Forbear! be calm, my lady. I married her this morning to Mr Granville Wharton.'

She set her lips, looked more intently at me than ever, raised her right hand, and smote me hard upon the cheek.

'Give me back those papers! give me back those papers!' She tore them out of my hands, and tossed them on her table. Then seating herself defiantly in her great chair, and folding her arms, she stabbed me to the heart with the unlooked-for reproach, 'You worldly wretch!'

'Worldly?' I cried. 'Worldly?'

'This, if you please,'—she went on with supreme scorn, pointing me out as if there were some one there to see,—'this, if you please, is the disinterested scholar, with not a design beyond his books! This, if you please, is the simple creature whom any one could overreach in a bargain! This, if you please, is Mr Silverman! Not of this world; not he! He has too much simplicity for this world's cunning. He has too much singleness of purpose to be a match for this world's double-dealing. What did he give you for it?'

'For what? And who?'

'How much,' she asked, bending forward in her great chair, and insultingly tapping the fingers of her right hand on the palm of her left,—'how much does Mr Granville Wharton pay you for getting him Adelina's money? What is the amount of your percentage upon Adelina's fortune? What were the terms of the agreement that you proposed to this boy when you, the Rev. George Silverman, licensed to marry, engaged to put him in possession of this girl? You made good terms for yourself, whatever they were. He would stand a poor chance against your keenness.'

Bewildered, horrified, stunned by this cruel perversion, I could not speak.

But I trust that I looked innocent, being so.

'Listen to me, shrewd hypocrite,' said my lady, whose anger increased as she gave it utterance; 'attend to my words, you cunning schemer, who have carried this plot through with such a practised double face that I have never suspected you. I had my projects for my daughter; projects for family connection; projects for fortune. You have thwarted them, and overreached me; but I am not one to be thwarted and overreached without retaliation. Do you mean to hold this living another month?'

'Do you deem it possible, Lady Fareway, that I can hold it another hour, under your injurious words?'

'Is it resigned, then?'

'It was mentally resigned, my lady, some minutes ago.'

Don't equivocate, sir. IS it resigned?'

'Unconditionally and entirely; and I would that I had never, never come near it!'

'A cordial response from me to THAT wish, Mr Silverman! But take this with you, sir. If you had not resigned it, I would have had you deprived of it. And though you have resigned it, you will not get quit of me as easily as you think for. I will pursue you with this story. I will make this nefarious conspiracy of yours, for money, known. You have made money by it, but you have at the same time made an enemy by it. YOU will take good care that the money sticks to you; I will take good care that the enemy sticks to you.'

Then said I finally, 'Lady Fareway, I think my heart is broken. Until I came into this room just now, the possibility of such mean wickedness as you have imputed to me never dawned upon my thoughts. Your suspicions—'

'Suspicions! Pah!' said she indignantly. 'Certainties.'

'Your certainties, my lady, as you call them, your suspicions as I call them, are cruel, unjust, wholly devoid of foundation in fact. I can declare no more; except that I have not acted for my own profit or my own pleasure. I have not in this proceeding considered myself. Once again, I think my heart is broken. If I have unwittingly done any wrong with a righteous motive, that is some penalty to pay.'

She received this with another and more indignant 'Pah!' and I made my way out of her room (I think I felt my way out with my hands, although my eyes were open), almost suspecting that my voice had a repulsive sound, and that I was a repulsive object.

There was a great stir made, the bishop was appealed to, I received a severe reprimand, and narrowly escaped suspension. For years a cloud hung over me, and my name was tarnished.

But my heart did not break, if a broken heart involves death; for I lived through it.

They stood by me, Adelina and her husband, through it all. Those who had known me at college, and even most of those who had only known me there by reputation, stood by me too. Little by little, the belief widened that I was not capable of what was laid to my charge. At length I was presented to a college-living in a sequestered place, and there I now pen my explanation. I pen it at my open window in the summer-time, before me, lying in the churchyard, equal resting-place for sound hearts, wounded hearts, and broken hearts. I pen it for the relief of my own mind, not foreseeing whether or no it will ever have a reader.

7

THE POOR RELATION'S STORY

He was very reluctant to take precedence of so many respected members of the family, by beginning the round of stories they were to relate as they sat in a goodly circle by the Christmas fire; and he modestly suggested that it would be more correct if 'John our esteemed host' (whose health he begged to drink) would have the kindness to begin. For as to himself, he said, he was so little used to lead the way that really—. But as they all cried out here, that he must begin, and agreed with one voice that he might, could, would, and should begin, he left off rubbing his hands, and took his legs out from under his armchair, and did begin.

I have no doubt (said the poor relation) that I shall surprise the assembled members of our family, and particularly John our esteemed host to whom we are so much indebted for the great hospitality with which he has this day entertained us, by the confession I am going to make. But, if you do me the honour to be surprised at anything that falls from a person so unimportant in the family as I am, I can only say that I shall be scrupulously accurate in all I relate.

I am not what I am supposed to be. I am quite another thing. Perhaps before I go further, I had better glance at what I am supposed to be.

It is supposed, unless I mistake—the assembled members of

our family will correct me if I do, which is very likely (here the poor relation looked mildly about him for contradiction); that I am nobody's enemy but my own. That I never met with any particular success in anything. That I failed in business because I was unbusiness-like and credulous—in not being prepared for the interested designs of my partner. That I failed in love, because I was ridiculously trustful—in thinking it impossible that Christiana could deceive me. That I failed in my expectations from my uncle Chill, on account of not being as sharp as he could have wished in worldly matters. That, through life, I have been rather put upon and disappointed in a general way. That I am at present a bachelor of between fifty-nine and sixty years of age, living on a limited income in the form of a quarterly allowance, to which I see that John our esteemed host wishes me to make no further allusion.

The supposition as to my present pursuits and habits is to the following effect.

I live in a lodging in the Clapham Road—a very clean back room, in a very respectable house—where I am expected not to be at home in the day-time, unless poorly; and which I usually leave in the morning at nine o'clock, on pretence of going to business. I take my breakfast—my roll and butter, and my half-pint of coffee—at the old-established coffee-shop near Westminster Bridge; and then I go into the City—I don't know why—and sit in Garraway's Coffee House, and on 'Change, and walk about, and look into a few offices and counting-houses where some of my relations or acquaintance are so good as to tolerate me, and where I stand by the fire if the weather happens to be cold. I get through the day in this way until five o'clock, and then I dine: at a cost, on the average, of one and threepence. Having still a little money to spend on my evening's entertainment, I look into the old-established coffee-shop as I go home, and take my cup of tea, and perhaps my bit of toast. So, as the large hand of the clock makes its way round to the morning hour again, I make my way round to the Clapham Road again, and go to bed when I get to my lodging—fire being expensive, and being objected to by the family on account of its giving trouble and making a dirt.

Sometimes, one of my relations or acquaintances is so obliging as to ask me to dinner. Those are holiday occasions, and then I generally walk in the Park. I am a solitary man, and seldom walk with anybody. Not that I am avoided because I am shabby; for I am not at all shabby, having always a very good suit of black on (or rather Oxford mixture, which has the appearance of black and wears much better); but I have got into a habit of speaking low, and being rather silent, and my spirits are not high, and I am sensible that I am not an attractive companion.

The only exception to this general rule is the child of my first cousin, Little Frank. I have a particular affection for that child, and he takes very kindly to me. He is a diffident boy by nature; and in a crowd he is soon run over, as I may say, and forgotten. He and I, however, get on exceedingly well. I have a fancy that the poor child will in time succeed to my peculiar position in the family. We talk but little; still, we understand each other. We walk about, hand in hand; and without much speaking he knows what I mean, and I know what he means. When he was very little indeed, I used to take him to the windows of the toy-shops, and show him the toys inside. It is surprising how soon he found out that I would have made him a great many presents if I had been in circumstances to do it.

Little Frank and I go and look at the outside of the Monument—he is very fond of the Monument—and at the Bridges, and at all the sights that are free. On two of my birthdays, we have dined on a-la-mode beef, and gone at half-price to the play, and been deeply interested. I was once walking with him in Lombard Street, which we often visit on account of my having mentioned to him that there are great riches there—he is very fond of Lombard Street—when a gentleman said to me as he passed by, 'Sir, your little son has dropped his glove.' I assure you, if you will excuse my remarking on so trivial a circumstance, this accidental mention of the child as mine, quite touched my heart and brought the foolish tears into my eyes.

When Little Frank is sent to school in the country, I shall be very much at a loss what to do with myself, but I have the intention of walking down there once a month and seeing him on a half holiday. I am told he will then be at play upon the Heath; and if my visits should be objected to, as unsettling the child, I can see him from a distance without his seeing me, and walk back again. His mother comes of a highly genteel family, and rather disapproves, I am aware, of our being too much together. I know that I am not calculated to improve his retiring disposition; but I think he would miss me beyond the feeling of the moment if we were wholly separated.

When I die in the Clapham Road, I shall not leave much more in this world than I shall take out of it; but, I happen to have a miniature of a bright-faced boy, with a curling head, and an open shirt-frill waving down his bosom (my mother had it taken for me, but I can't believe that it was ever liked), which will be worth nothing to sell, and which I shall beg may be given to Frank. I have written my dear boy a little letter with it, in which I have told him that I felt very sorry to part from him, though bound to confess that I knew no reason why I should remain here. I have given him some short advice, the best in my power, to take warning of the consequences of being nobody's enemy but his own; and I have endeavoured to comfort him for what I fear he will consider a bereavement, by pointing out to him, that I was only a superfluous something to every one but him; and that having by some means failed to find a place in this great assembly, I am better out of it.

Such (said the poor relation, clearing his throat and beginning to speak a little louder) is the general impression about me. Now, it is a remarkable circumstance which forms the aim and purpose of my story, that this is all wrong. This is not my life, and these are not my habits. I do not even live in the Clapham Road. Comparatively speaking, I am very seldom there. I reside, mostly, in a—I am almost ashamed to say the word, it sounds so full of pretension—in a Castle. I do not mean that it is an old baronial habitation, but still it is a building always known to every one by the name of a Castle. In it, I preserve the particulars of my history; they run thus:

It was when I first took John Spatter (who had been my clerk) into partnership, and when I was still a young man of not more than five-and-twenty, residing in the house of my uncle Chill, from whom I had considerable expectations, that I ventured to propose to Christiana. I had loved Christiana a long time. She was very beautiful, and very winning in all respects. I rather mistrusted her widowed mother, who I feared was of a plotting and mercenary turn of mind; but, I thought as well of her as I could, for Christiana's sake. I never had loved any one but Christiana, and she had been all the world, and far more than all the world, to me, from our childhood!

Christiana accepted me with her mother's consent, and I was rendered very happy indeed. My life at my uncle Chill's was of a spare dull kind, and my garret chamber was as dull, and bare, and cold, as an upper prison room in some stern northern fortress. But, having Christiana's love, I wanted nothing upon earth. I would not have changed my lot with any human being.

Avarice was, unhappily, my uncle Chill's master-vice. Though he was rich, he pinched, and scraped, and clutched, and lived miserably. As Christiana had no fortune, I was for some time a little fearful of confessing our engagement to him; but, at length I wrote him a letter, saying how it all truly was. I put it into his hand one night, on going to bed.

As I came down-stairs next morning, shivering in the cold December air; colder in my uncle's unwarmed house than in the street, where the winter sun did sometimes shine, and which was at all events enlivened by cheerful faces and voices passing along; I carried a heavy heart towards the long, low breakfast-room in which my uncle sat. It was a large room with a small fire, and there was a great bay window in it which the rain had marked in the night as if with the tears of houseless people. It stared upon a raw yard, with a cracked stone pavement, and some rusted iron railings half uprooted, whence an ugly out-building that had once been a dissecting-room (in the time of the great surgeon who had mortgaged the house to my uncle), stared at it.

We rose so early always, that at that time of the year we breakfasted by candle-light. When I went into the room, my uncle was so contracted by the cold, and so huddled together in his chair behind the one dim candle, that I did not see him until I was close to the table.

As I held out my hand to him, he caught up his stick (being infirm, he always walked about the house with a stick), and made a blow at me, and said, 'You fool!'

'Uncle,' I returned, 'I didn't expect you to be so angry as this.' Nor had I expected it, though he was a hard and angry old man.

'You didn't expect!' said he; 'When did you ever expect? When did you ever calculate, or look forward, you contemptible dog?'

'These are hard words, uncle!'

'Hard words? Feathers, to pelt such an idiot as you with,' said he. 'Here! Betsy Snap! Look at him!'

Betsy Snap was a withered, hard-favoured, yellow old woman—our only domestic—always employed, at this time of the morning, in rubbing my uncle's legs. As my uncle adjured her to look at me, he put his lean grip on the crown of her head, she kneeling beside him, and turned her face towards me. An involuntary thought connecting them both with the Dissecting Room, as it must often have been in the surgeon's time, passed across my mind in the midst of my anxiety.

'Look at the snivelling milksop!' said my uncle. 'Look at the baby! This is the gentleman who, people say, is nobody's enemy but his own. This is the gentleman who can't say no. This is the gentleman who was making such large profits in his business that he must needs take a partner, t'other day. This is the gentleman who is going to marry a wife without a penny, and who falls into the hands of Jezabels who are speculating on my death!'

I knew, now, how great my uncle's rage was; for nothing short of his being almost beside himself would have induced him to utter that concluding word, which he held in such repugnance that it was never spoken or hinted at before him on any account.

'On my death,' he repeated, as if he were defying me by defying his own abhorrence of the word. 'On my death—death—Death! But I'll spoil the speculation. Eat your last under this roof, you feeble wretch, and may it choke you!'

You may suppose that I had not much appetite for the breakfast to which I was bidden in these terms; but, I took my accustomed seat. I saw that I was repudiated henceforth by my uncle; still I could bear that very well, possessing Christiana's heart.

He emptied his basin of bread and milk as usual, only that he took it on his knees with his chair turned away from the table where I sat. When he had done, he carefully snuffed out the candle; and the cold, slate-coloured, miserable day looked in upon us.

'Now, Mr Michael,' said he, 'before we part, I should like to have a word with these ladies in your presence.'

'As you will, sir,' I returned; 'but you deceive yourself, and wrong us, cruelly, if you suppose that there is any feeling at stake in this contract but pure, disinterested, faithful love.'

To this, he only replied, 'You lie!' and not one other word.

We went, through half-thawed snow and half-frozen rain, to the house where Christiana and her mother lived. My uncle knew them very well. They were sitting at their breakfast, and were surprised to see us at that hour.

'Your servant, ma'am,' said my uncle to the mother. 'You divine the purpose of my visit, I dare say, ma'am. I understand there is a world of pure, disinterested, faithful love cooped up here. I am happy to bring it all it wants, to make it complete. I bring you your son-in-law, ma'am—and you, your husband, miss. The gentleman is a perfect stranger to me, but I wish him joy of his wise bargain.'

He snarled at me as he went out, and I never saw him again.

It is altogether a mistake (continued the poor relation) to suppose that my dear Christiana, over-persuaded and influenced by her mother, married a rich man, the dirt from whose carriage wheels is often, in these changed times, thrown upon me as she rides by. No, no. She married me.

The way we came to be married rather sooner than we intended, was this. I took a frugal lodging and was saving and planning for her sake, when, one day, she spoke to me with great earnestness, and said:

'My dear Michael, I have given you my heart. I have said that I loved you, and I have pledged myself to be your wife. I am as much yours through all changes of good and evil as if we had been married on the day when such words passed between us. I know you well, and know that if we should be separated and our union broken off, your whole life would be shadowed, and all that might, even now, be stronger in your character for the conflict with the world would then be weakened to the shadow of what it is!'

'God help me, Christiana!' said I. 'You speak the truth.'

'Michael!' said she, putting her hand in mine, in all maidenly devotion, 'Let us keep apart no longer. It is but for me to say that I can live contented upon such means as you have, and I well know you are happy. I say so from my heart. Strive no more alone; let us strive together. My dear Michael, it is not right that I should keep secret from you what you do not suspect, but what distresses my whole life. My mother: without considering that what you have lost, you have lost for me, and on the assurance of my faith: sets her heart on riches, and urges another suit upon me, to my misery. I cannot bear this, for to bear it is to be untrue to you. I would rather share your struggles than look on. I want no better home than you can give me. I know that you will aspire and labour with a higher courage if I am wholly yours, and let it be so when you will!'

I was blest indeed, that day, and a new world opened to me. We were married in a very little while, and I took my wife to our happy home. That was the beginning of the residence I have spoken of; the Castle we have ever since inhabited together, dates from that time. All our children have been born in it. Our first child—now married—was a little girl, whom we called Christiana. Her son is so like Little Frank, that I hardly know which is which.

The current impression as to my partner's dealings with me is also quite erroneous. He did not begin to treat me coldly, as a poor simpleton, when my uncle and I so fatally quarrelled; nor did he afterwards gradually possess himself of our business and edge me out. On the contrary, he behaved to me with the utmost good faith and honour.

Matters between us took this turn:- On the day of my separation from my uncle, and even before the arrival at our counting-house of my trunks (which he sent after me, NOT carriage paid), I went down to our room of business, on our little wharf, overlooking the river; and there I told John Spatter what had happened. John did not say, in reply, that rich old relatives were palpable facts, and that love and sentiment were moonshine and fiction. He addressed me thus:

'Michael,' said John, 'we were at school together, and I generally had the knack of getting on better than you, and making a higher reputation.'

'You had, John,' I returned.

'Although' said John, 'I borrowed your books and lost them; borrowed your pocket-money, and never repaid it; got you to buy my damaged knives at a higher price than I had given for them new; and to own to the windows that I had broken.'

'All not worth mentioning, John Spatter,' said I, 'but certainly true.'

'When you were first established in this infant business, which promises to thrive so well,' pursued John, 'I came to you, in my search for almost any employment, and you made me your clerk.'

'Still not worth mentioning, my dear John Spatter,' said I; 'still, equally true.'

'And finding that I had a good head for business, and that I was really useful to the business, you did not like to retain me in that capacity, and thought it an act of justice soon to make me your partner.'

'Still less worth mentioning than any of those other little circumstances you have recalled, John Spatter,' said I; 'for I was, and am, sensible of your merits and my deficiencies.'

'Now, my good friend,' said John, drawing my arm through his, as he had had a habit of doing at school; while two vessels outside the windows of our counting-house—which were shaped like the stern windows of a ship—went lightly down the river with the tide, as John and I might then be sailing away in company, and in trust and confidence, on our voyage of life; 'let there, under these friendly circumstances, be a right understanding between us. You are too easy, Michael. You are nobody's enemy but your own. If I were to give you that damaging character among our connexion, with a shrug, and a shake of the head, and a sigh; and if I were further to abuse the trust you place in me—'

'But you never will abuse it at all, John,' I observed.

'Never!' said he; 'but I am putting a case—I say, and if I were further to abuse that trust by keeping this piece of our common affairs in the dark, and this other piece in the light, and again this other piece in the twilight, and so on, I should strengthen my strength, and weaken your weakness, day by day, until at last I found myself on the high road to fortune, and you left behind on some bare common, a hopeless number of miles out of the way.'

'Exactly so,' said I.

'To prevent this, Michael,' said John Spatter, 'or the remotest chance of this, there must be perfect openness between us. Nothing must be concealed, and we must have but one interest.'

'My dear, John Spatter,' I assured him, 'that is precisely what I mean.'

'And when you are too easy,' pursued John, his face glowing with friendship, 'you must allow me to prevent that imperfection in your nature from being taken advantage of, by any one; you must not expect me to humour it—'

'My dear, John Spatter,' I interrupted, 'I Don't expect you to humour it. I want to correct it.'

'And I, too,' said John.

'Exactly so!' cried I. 'We both have the same end in view; and, honourably seeking it, and fully trusting one another, and having but one interest, ours will be a prosperous and happy partnership.'

'I am sure of it!' returned John Spatter. And we shook hands most affectionately.

I took John home to my Castle, and we had a very happy day. Our partnership throve well. My friend and partner supplied what I wanted, as I had foreseen that he would, and by improving both the business and myself, amply acknowledged any little rise in life to which I had helped him.

I am not (said the poor relation, looking at the fire as he slowly rubbed his hands) very rich, for I never cared to be that; but I have enough, and am above all moderate wants and anxieties. My Castle is not a splendid place, but it is very comfortable, and it has a warm and cheerful air, and is quite a picture of Home.

Our eldest girl, who is very like her mother, married John Spatter's eldest son. Our two families are closely united in other ties of attachment. It is very pleasant of an evening, when we are all assembled together—which frequently happens—and when John and I talk over old times, and the one interest there has always been between us.

I really do not know, in my Castle, what loneliness is. Some of our children or grandchildren are always about it, and the young voices of my descendants are delightful—O, how delightful!—to me to hear. My dearest and most devoted wife, ever faithful, ever loving, ever helpful and sustaining and consoling, is the priceless blessing of my house; from whom all its other blessings spring. We are rather a musical family, and when Christiana sees me, at any time, a little weary or depressed, she steals to the piano and sings a gentle air she used to sing when we were first betrothed. So weak a man am I, that I cannot bear to hear it from any other source. They played it once, at the Theatre, when I was there with Little Frank; and the child said wondering, 'Cousin Michael, whose hot tears are these that have fallen on my hand!'

Such is my Castle, and such are the real particulars of my life therein preserved. I often take Little Frank home there. He is very welcome to my grandchildren, and they play together. At this time of the year—the Christmas and New Year time—I am seldom out of my Castle. For, the associations of the season seem to hold me there, and the precepts of the season seem to teach me that it is well to be there.

'And the Castle is—' observed a grave, kind voice among the company.

'Yes. My Castle,' said the poor relation, shaking his head as he still looked at the fire, 'is in the Air. John our esteemed host suggests its situation accurately. My Castle is in the Air! I have done. Will you be so good as to pass the story?'

8

THE BARON OF GROGSWIG

The Baron Von Koëldwethout, of Grogzwig in Germany, was as likely a young baron as you would wish to see. I needn't say that he lived in a castle, because that's of course; neither need I say that he lived in an old castle; for what German baron ever lived in a new one? There were many strange circumstances connected with this venerable building, among which, not the least startling and mysterious were, that when the wind blew, it rumbled in the chimneys, or even howled among the trees in the neighboring forest; and that when the moon shone, she found her way through certain small loopholes in the wall, and actually made some parts of the wide halls and galleries quite light, while she left others in gloomy shadow. I believe that one of the baron's ancestors, being short of money, had inserted a dagger in a gentleman who called one night to ask his way, and it was supposed that these miraculous occurrences took place in consequence. And yet I hardly know how that could have been, either, because the baron's ancestor, who was an amiable man, felt very sorry afterwards for having been so rash, and laying violent hands upon a quantity of stone and timber which belonged to a weaker baron, built a chapel as an apology, and so took a receipt from Heaven, in full of all demands.

Talking of the baron's ancestor puts me in mind of the baron's great claims to respect, on the score of his pedigree. I am afraid to say, I am sure, how many ancestors the baron had; but I know that he had a great many more than any other man of his time; and I only wish that he had lived in these latter days, that he might have had more. It is a very hard thing upon the great men of past centuries, that they should have come into the world so soon, because a man who was born three or four hundred years ago, cannot reasonably be expected to have had as many relations before him, as a man who is born now. The last man, whoever he is—and he may be a cobbler or some low vulgar dog for aught we know—will have a longer pedigree than the greatest nobleman now alive; and I contend that this is not fair.

Well, but the Baron Von Koëldwethout of Grogwig! He was a fine swarthy fellow, with dark hair and large moustachios, who rode a-hunting in clothes of Lincoln green, with russet boots on his feet, and a bugle slung over his shoulder, like the guard of a long stage. When he blew this bugle, four-and-twenty other gentlemen of inferior rank, in Lincoln green a little coarser, and russet boots with a little thicker soles, turned out directly; and away galloped the whole train, with spears in their hands like lackered area railings, to hunt down the boars, or perhaps encounter a bear: in which latter case the baron killed him first, and greased his whiskers with him afterwards.

This was a merry life for the Baron of Grogzwig, and merrier still for the baron's retainers, who drank Rhine wine every night till they fell under the table, and then had the bottles on the floor, and called for pipes. Never were such jolly, roystering, rollicking, merry-making blades, as the jovial crew of Grogzwig.

But the pleasures of the table, or the pleasures of under the table, require a little variety; especially when the same five-and-twenty people sit daily down to the same board, to discuss the same subjects, and tell the same stories. The baron grew weary, and wanted excitement. He took to quarrelling with his gentlemen, and tried kicking two or three of them every day after dinner. This was a pleasant change at first; but it became monotonous after a week or so, and the baron felt quite out of sorts, and cast about, in despair, for some new amusement.

One night, after a day's sport in which he had outdone Nimrod or Gillingwater, and slaughtered 'another fine bear', and brought him home in triumph, the Baron Von Koëldwethout sat moodily at the head of his table, eyeing the smoky roof of the hall with a discontented aspect. He swallowed huge bumpers of wine, but the more he swallowed, the more he frowned. The gentlemen who had been honoured with the dangerous distinction of sitting on his right and left, imitated him to a miracle in the drinking, and frowned at each other.

'I will!' cried the baron suddenly, smiting the table with his right hand, and twirling his moustache with his left. 'Fill to the Lady of Grogzwig!'

The four-and-twenty Lincoln greens turned pale, with the exception of their four-and-twenty noses, which were unchangeable.

'I said to the Lady of Grogzwig,' repeated the baron, looking round the board.

'To the Lady of Grogzwig!' shouted the Lincoln greens; and down their four-and-twenty throats went four-and-twenty imperial pints of such rare old hock, that they smacked their eight-and-forty lips, and winked again.

'The fair daughter of the Baron Von Swillenhausen,' said Koëldwethout, condescending to explain. 'We will demand her in marriage of her father, ere the sun goes down tomorrow. If he refuse our suit, we will cut off his nose.'

A hoarse murmur arose from the company; every man touched, first the hilt of his sword, and then the tip of his nose, with appalling significance.

What a pleasant thing filial piety is, to contemplate! If the daughter of the Baron Von Swillenhausen had pleaded a preoccupied heart, or fallen at her father's feet and corned them in salt tears, or only fainted away, and complimented the old gentleman in frantic ejaculations, the odds are a hundred to one, but Swillenhausen castle would have been turned out at window, or rather the baron turned out at window, and the castle demolished. The damsel held her peace, however, when an early messenger bore the request of Von Koëldwethout next morning, and modestly retired to her chamber, from the casement of which she watched the coming of the suitor and his retinue. She was no sooner assured that the horseman with the large moustachios was her proferred husband, than she hastened to her father's presence, and expressed her readiness to sacrifice herself to secure his peace. The venerable baron caught his child into his arms, and shed a wink of joy.

There was a great feasting at the castle, that day. The four-and-twenty Lincoln greens of Von Koëldwethout exchanged vows of eternal friendship with twelve Lincoln greens of Von Swillenhausen, and promised the old baron that they would drink his wine 'Till all was blue'—meaning probably until their whole countenances had acquired the same tint as their noses. Everybody slapped everybody else's back, when the time for parting came; and the Baron Von Koëldwethout and his followers rode gaily home.

For six mortal weeks, the bears and boars had a holiday. The houses of Koëldwethout and Swillenhausen were united; the spears rusted; and the baron's bugle grew hoarse for lack of blowing.

Those were great times for the four-and-twenty; but, alas! their high and palmy days had taken boots to themselves, and were already walking off.

'My dear,' said the baroness.

'My love,' said the baron.

'Those coarse, noisy men—'

'Which, ma'am?' said the baron starting.

The baroness pointed, from the window at which they stood, to the courtyard beneath, where the unconscious Lincoln greens were taking a copious stirrup-cup, preparatory to issuing forth, after a boar or two.

'My hunting train, ma'am,' said the baron.

'Disband them, love,' murmured the baroness.

'Disband them!' cried the baron, in amazement.

'To please me, love,' replied the baroness.

'To please the devil, ma'am,' answered the baron.

Whereupon the baroness uttered a great cry, and swooned away at the baron's feet.

What could the baron do? He called for the lady's maid, and roared for the doctor; and then, rushing into the yard, kicked the two Lincoln greens who were the most used to it, and cursing the others all round, bade them go—but never mind where, I don't know the German for it, or I would put it delicately that way.

It is not for me to say by what means or by what degrees, some wives manage to keep down some husbands as they do, although I may have my private opinion on the subject, and may think that no Member of Parliament ought to be married, in as much as three married members out of every four, must vote according to their wives' consciences if there be such things, and not according to their own. All I need say, just now, is, that the Baroness Von Koëldwethout somehow or other acquired great control over the Baron Von Koëldwethout, and that, little by little, and bit by bit, and day by day, and year by year, the baron got the worst of some disputed question, or was slily unhorsed from some old hobby; and that by the time he was a fat hearty fellow of forty-eight or thereabouts, he had no feasting, no revelry, no hunting train, and no hunting—nothing in short that he liked, or used to have; and that, although he was as fierce as a lion and as bold as brass, he was decidedly snubbed and put down, by his own lady, in his own castle of Grogzwig.

Nor was this the whole extent of the baron's misfortunes. About a year after his nuptials, there came into the world a lusty young baron, in whose honour a great many fireworks were let off, and a great many dozens of wine drunk; but next year there came a young baroness, and next year another young baron, and so on, every year, either a baron or baroness and one year both together, until the baron found himself the father of a small family of twelve. Upon every one of these anniversaries, the venerable Baroness Von Swillenhausen was nervously sensitive for the well-being of her child the Baroness Von Koëldwethout and although it was not found that the good lady ever did anything material towards contributing to her child's recovery, still she made it a point of duty to be as nervous as possible at the castle at Grogzwig, and to divide her time between moral observations on the baron's housekeeping, and bewailing the hard lot of her unhappy daughter. And if the Baron of Grogzwig, a little hurt and irritated at this, took heart, and ventured to suggest that his wife was at least no worse off than the wives of other barons, the Baroness Von Swillenhausen begged all persons to take notice, that nobody but she, sympathized with her dear daughter's sufferings; upon which, her relations and friends remarked, that to be sure she did cry a great deal more than her son-in-law, and that if there were a hard-hearted brute alive, it was that Baron of Grogzwig.

The poor baron bore it all, as long as he could, and when he could bear it no longer lost his appetite and his spirits, and sat himself gloomily and dejectedly down. But there were worse troubles yet in store for him, and as they came on, his melancholy and sadness increased. Times changed. He got into debt. The Grogzwig coffers ran low, though the Swillenhausen family had looked upon them as inexhaustible; and just when the baroness was on the point of making a thirteenth addition to the family pedigree, Von Koëldwethout discovered that he had no means of replenishing them.

'I don't see what is to be done,' said the baron. 'I think, I'll kill myself.'

This was a bright idea. The baron took an old hunting-knife

from a cupboard hard by, and having sharpened it on his boot, made what boys call 'an offer' at his throat.

'Hem!' said the baron, stopping short. 'Perhaps it's not sharp enough.'

The baron sharpened it again, and made another offer, when his hand was arrested by a loud screaming among the young barons and baronesses, who had a nursery in an upstairs tower with iron bars outside the window, to prevent their tumbling out into the moat.

'If I had been a bachelor,' said the baron sighing, 'I might have done it fifty times over, without being interrupted. Hallo! Put a flask of wine and the largest pipe, in the little vaulted room behind the hall.'

One of the domestics, in a very kind manner, executed the baron's order in the course of half an hour or so, and Von Koëldwethout being apprised thereof, strode to the vaulted room, the walls of which, being of dark shining wood, gleamed in the light of the blazing logs which were piled upon the hearth. The bottle and pipe were ready, and, upon the whole, the place looked very comfortable.

'Leave the lamp,' said the baron.

'Anything else, my lord?' inquired the domestic.

'The room,' replied the baron. The domestic obeyed, and the baron locked the door.

'I'll smoke a last pipe,' said the baron, 'and then I'll be off.' So, putting the knife upon the table till he wanted it, and tossing off a goodly measure of wine, the Lord of Grogzwig threw himself back in his chair, stretched his legs out before the fire, and puffed away.

He thought about a great many things—about his present troubles and past days of bachelorship, and about the Lincoln greens, long since disappeared up and down the country, no one knew whither: with the exception of two who had been unfortunately beheaded, and four who had killed themselves with drinking. His mind was running upon bears and boars, when, in the process of draining his glass to the bottom, he raised his eyes, and saw, for the first time and with unbounded astonishment, that he was not alone.

No, he was not; for, on the opposite side of the fire, there sat with folded arms a wrinkled hideous figure, with deeply sunk and bloodshot eyes, and an immensely long, cadaverous face, shadowed by jagged and matted locks of coarse black hair. He wore a kind of tunic of a dull bluish colour, which, the baron observed, on regarding it attentively, was clasped or ornamented down the front, with coffin handles. His legs too, were encased in coffin plates as though in armour; and over his left shoulder he wore a short dusky cloak, which seemed made of remnant of some pall. He took no notice of the baron, but was intently eyeing the fire.

'Halloa!' said the baron, stamping his foot to attract attention.

'Halloa!' replied the stranger, moving his eyes towards the baron, but not his face or himself. 'What now?'

'What now?' replied the baron, nothing daunted by his hollow voice and lustreless eyes, 'I should ask that question. How did you get here?'

'Through the door,' replied the figure.

'What are you?' says the baron.

'A man,' replied the figure.

'I don't believe it,' says the baron.

'Disbelieve it then,' says the figure.

'I will,' rejoined the baron.

The figure looked at the bold Baron of Grogzwig for some time, and then said familiarly,

'There's no coming over you, I see. I'm not a man!'

'What are you then?' asked the baron.

'A genius,' replied the figure.

'You don't look much like one,' returned the baron scornfully.

'I am the Genius of Despair and Suicide,' said the apparition. 'Now you know me.'

With these words the apparition turned towards the baron, as if composing himself for a talk—and, what was very remarkable, was, that he threw his cloak aside, and displaying a stake, which was run through the centre of his body, pulled it out with a jerk, and laid it on the table, as composedly as if it had been a walking-stick.

'Now,' said the figure, glancing at the hunting-knife, 'are you ready for me?'

'Not quite,' rejoined the baron; 'I must finish this pipe first.'

'Look sharp then,' said the figure.

You seem in a hurry,' said the baron.

'Why, yes, I am,' answered the figure; 'they're doing a pretty brisk business in my way, over in England and France just now, and my time is a good deal taken up.'

'Do you drink?' said the baron, touching the bottle with the bowl of his pipe.

'Nine times out of ten, and then very hard,' rejoined the figure, drily.

'Never in moderation?' asked the baron.

'Never,' replied the figure, with a shudder, 'that breeds cheerfulness.'

The baron took another look at his new friend, whom he thought an uncommonly queer customer, and at length inquired whether he took any active part in such little proceedings as that which he had in contemplation.

'No,' replied the figure evasively; 'but I am always present.'

'Just to see fair, I suppose?' said the baron.

'Just that,' replied the figure playing with the stake, and examining the ferule.

'Be as quick as you can, will you, for there's a young gentleman who is afflicted with too much money and leisure wanting me now, I find.'

'Going to kill himself because he has too much money!' exclaimed the baron, quite tickled: 'Ha! ha! That's a good one.' This was the first time the baron had laughed for many a long day.

'I say,' expostulated the figure, looking very much scared; 'don't do that again.'

'Why not?' demanded the baron.

'Because it gives me pain all over,' replied the figure. 'sigh as much as you please; that does me good.'

The baron sighed mechanically, at the mention of the word; the figure, brightening up again, handed him the hunting-knife with the most winning politeness.

'It's not a bad idea though,' said the baron, feeling the edge of the weapon; 'a man killing himself because he has too much money.'

'Pooh!' said the apparition, petulantly, 'no better than a man's killing himself because he has none or little.'

Whether the genius unintentionally committed himself in saying this, or whether he thought the baron's mind was so thoroughly made up that it didn't matter what he said, I have no means of knowing. I only know that the baron stopped his hand, all of a sudden, opened his eyes wide, and looked as if quite a new light had come upon him for the first time.

'Why, certainly,' said Von Koëldwethout, 'nothing is too bad to be retrieved.'

'Except empty coffers,' cried the genius.

'Well, but they may be one day filled again,' said the baron.

'Scolding wives,' snarled the genius.

'Oh! They may be made quiet,' said the baron.

'Thirteen children,' shouted the genius.

'Can't all go wrong, surely,' said the baron.

The genius was evidently growing very savage with the baron, for holding these opinions all at once; but he tried to laugh it off, and said if he would let him know when he had left off joking, he should feel obliged to him.

'But I am not joking; I was never farther from it,' remonstrated the baron.

'Well, I am glad to hear that,' said the genius, looking very grim, 'because a joke, without any figure of speech, is the death of me. Come! Quit this dreary world at once.'

'I don't know,' said the baron, playing with the knife; 'it's a dreary one certainly, but I don't think yours is much better, for you have not the appearance of being particularly comfortable. That puts me in mind—what security have I, that I shall be any the better for going out of the world after all!' he cried, starting up; 'I never thought of that.'

'Dispatch,' cried the figure, gnashing its teeth.

'Keep off!' said the baron, 'I'll brood over miseries no longer, but put a good face on the matter, and try the fresh air and the bears again; and if that don't do, I'll talk to the baroness soundly, and cut the Von Swillenhausens dead.' With this the baron fell into his chair, and laughed so loud and boisterously, that the room rang with it.

The figure fell back a pace or two, regarding the baron meanwhile with a look of intense terror, and when he had ceased, caught up the stake, plunged it violently into its body, uttered a frightful howl, and disappeared.

Von Koëldwethout never saw it again. Having once made up his mind to action, he soon brought the baroness and the Von Swillenhausens to reason, and died many years afterwards; not a rich man that I am aware of, but certainly a happy one: leaving behind him a numerous family, who had been carefully educated in bear and boar-hunting under his own personal eye. And my advice to all men is, that if ever they become hipped and melancholy from similar causes as very many men do, they look at both sides of the question, applying a magnifying glass to the best one; and if they still feel tempted to retire without leave, that they smoke a large pipe and drink a full bottle first, and profit by the laudable example of the Baron of Grogzwig.

ABOUT TERRY O'BRIEN

Terry O'Brien is an academic with three decades of experience in teaching language and communication skills in India and abroad. He also headed a college under the auspices of the University of Delhi.

A prolific writer, with several books to his credit, Terry O'Brien is a reputed professional motivational speaker and a quizmaster.